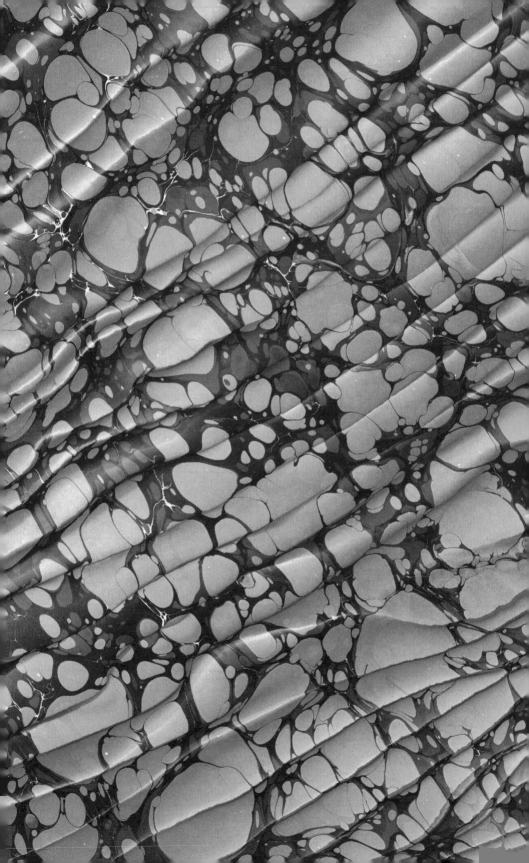

ANN JUNGMAN

Lucy Keeps the Wolf from the Door

Illustrated by Karin Littlewood

Young Lions
An Imprint of HarperCollinsPublishers

For Nicola and Fiona

First published in Great Britain in Young Lions 1989
Second impression April 1992

Young Lions is an imprint of
HarperCollins Children's Books,
a division of HarperCollins Publishers Ltd,
77–85 Fulham Palace Road,
Hammersmith, London W6 8JB

ISBN 0 00 673050 7

Printed and bound in Great Britain by
HarperCollins Manufacturing, Glasgow

1

The Triplets

Lucy was walking home from school one day when she saw 2.15 racing along the path towards her.

'Congratulate me,' he cried, jumping up and down with excitement. 'I wanted you to be the first to know that I'm a father,' said the wolf proudly. '3.45 had three cubs today.'

Lucy gave him a big hug. '2.15, that's wonderful! You must feel very happy.'

'I do,' said the wolf, 'I really do.'

'Why don't you come home with me,' suggested Lucy, 'and tell Gran and Grandad?'

'No, I can't,' said 2.15. 'I've got new responsibilities now. I've got to take care of 3.45 and the little ones, but I did want you to know.'

'I'll tell everyone,' said Lucy. 'I'll be around at Gran's tonight. You come if you can manage it.'

'The little house on the edge of the village?' asked 2.15. 'Good, I've got yer. See you later.'

'Love to 3.45 and the cubs,' called Lucy. 'Byee.'

Gran and Grandad were delighted when they heard the news.

'Three!' said Gran. 'Oh, that is nice. I can't wait to see them.'

'Well,' commented Grandad, ' 'e certainly has done well. I'm going right out to get a bottle of Champagne for when 'e comes round to celebrate.'

'Come off it, Bert,' said Gran, 'we can't afford Champagne. We've got to manage on our pensions, remember.'

'Pension or no pension,' replied Grandad, '2.15 is my mate and 'e's gone and 'ad triplets and the least we can do is celebrate in style.'

So later that evening Gran, Grandad, Lucy and Lucy's Mum and Dad sat round the kitchen table and waited for 2.15.

'Maybe he won't be able to get away,' said Lucy wistfully. 'I do hope he does. I do want him to know how pleased we all are.'

'Fear not faint hearted one,' came 2.15's voice and he leapt in through the window. 'I am here as I promised though for a brief moment only, as I must return to my duties as a father shortly.'

Grandad leapt up and shook 2.15's paw and Lucy's Mum gave him a big kiss.

'I went out and bought Champagne for us to celebrate proper like,' Grandad told the wolf proudly.

'Dear friend,' said the wolf fondly. 'You are too kind and you should save your money for necessary things.'

'Least I could do,' insisted Grandad. 'After all, if it wasn't for you we wouldn't be sitting here now.'

Grandad filled the six glasses with Champagne.

'Who's going to propose the toast?' asked Gran.

'Why not you?' suggested 2.15. 'After all, the Grannie is a pretty important person in the story of Red Riding Hood. But hold a moment. Where are my good friends Pete and Lily Grubb?'

'We didn't invite them,' Lucy told him. 'We didn't think you'd want to see them.'

'Of course I want them here,' replied the wolf. 'They are old friends, well, old acquaintances anyway. Let the fair Lily and the dreadful Pete join us in a glass of good cheer.'

6

'I'll go and get them,' said Lucy's Dad. 'I'll be back in a minute. I know 2.15 is in a hurry.'

A few minutes later the Grubbs trundled into the room and joined the group.

'I hear you're to be congratulated, 2.15,' said Pete Grubb sourly. 'So now there's three more like you to make my life miserable.'

'That's the only reason they're here, Mr Grubb,' replied 2.15 cheerfully.

'Don't be such a misery, Pete,' Lily Grubb reproved him. 'This is a happy occasion. Congratulations, 2.15, and to 3.45 too.'

'Well, I don't know,' mumbled Pete Grubb. 'Where's this Champagne, then?'

So two more glasses were poured and Gran stood up.

'Friends, I have been asked to propose a toast to 2.15,

3.45 and their three new cubs. 2.15, I want you to know how happy we are to have three new young furry friends living near us and we all hope to see a lot of them and that your new responsibilities will not keep you from us or stop you trying to see to it that we all live happily ever after. Friends, I give you 2.15, 3.45 and the cubs.'

'2.15, 3.45 and the cubs,' chorused everyone, raising their glasses.

'Thank you, thank you,' cried 2.15. 'Dear friends, you are all very kind. I hope you will make a sortie into the forest and see 3.45 and my little ones in the near future, except Mr Grubb that is, who might upset my 3.45 just the tiniest, weeniest bit.'

'I don't want to go,' declared Pete Grubb. 'Wild horses wouldn't get me there. Don't you worry about that.'

So the next day Lucy and Gran went walking in the forest, calling out for 2.15. Eventually they heard a scuffle and there stood 2.15 with a cub in his arms.

'Look,' he said proudly. 'This one is my little girl cub. Come on, 3.45 is waiting for you with the others.'

They found 3.45 lying under a tree with the two little cubs suckling.

'3.45,' cried Lucy. 'You're so clever! Congratulations!'

'It's nothing,' sniffed 3.45. 'All wolves do it. Nothing special about me. No need to make a fuss.'

'I'm not making a fuss,' said Lucy, feeling a bit hurt, 'I'm just pleased.'

'Come, let us go and sit under the branches of yonder spreading chestnut tree and have a talk. I need your advice on a matter of some urgency,' said 2.15.

As they sat down on the grass, 3.45 glared at them in a hostile way:

'Don't you give him any help or you'll have me to answer to.'

'Nonsense, my sweet one, nonsense,' said 2.15 amicably. 'All I want to know is what happens when children are born? What kind of a celebration do people have?'

'A christening usually,' said Gran. 'You go to church and the vicar gives the baby a name.'

'Then that is what we shall do,' declared 2.15. 'Pray tell me where I may find the vicar and request him to give my babies nice names?'

'You can't do that,' protested Gran. 'The whole village will get to know about you living in the forest.'

'The time has come for that,' replied 2.15. 'My cubs will need to be educated and to mingle with the rest of the world.'

'Well, all right,' said Gran dubiously, 'but I'm not at all sure that this is a good idea.'

So later that day Lucy and Grandad trudged round to see the vicar. Grandad rang the bell of the vicarage and waited.

'I don't know what I'm goin' to say to 'im,' muttered Grandad. ' 'e'll think I've gone clear round the bend when I ask 'im if 'e's got any objections to christenin' three cubs with a fairy-tale wolf for a father.'

Just then the door opened and there stood the Reverend Bell beaming at Lucy and Grandad.

'Come in,' he cried. 'Lovely to see you, Lucy, and you must be Mr Wood. It's always a pleasure to meet new parishioners.'

So over a cup of tea Lucy and Grandad told him the story of 2.15 and 3.45 and how they lived in the forest and wanted their three cubs christened.

'How wonderful,' he declared. 'How simply wonderful. I feel the Lord has blessed me by letting these wonderful creatures live within my parish. Yes, tell 2.15 I would be honoured and delighted to christen his triplets.'

9

So a date for a Saturday three weeks ahead was fixed. 2.15 was delighted when he heard.

'Good, good,' he cried. 'Now, in anticipation of the success of your venture I have made out a guest list of the people I would like you to invite to the celebration.'

Grandad looked at the list and his face fell. On it were the names of Sir Samuel and Lady Wolf, all the lads who had helped rescue 3.45, the dogs they had adopted, Liz Howes the social worker, Mr and Mrs Al-u-Din and their children, all the children from the flats and their parents and Gaston Loup.

'Who's Gaston Loup?' asked Grandad.

'The French onion seller whose clothes I borrowed. It's not his real name but it's what I like to call him.'

'But 'e lives in France.'

'Never mind,' said 2.15 patiently. 'Send him an invitation anyway. He doesn't have to come if it's too far but he might like to be invited.'

So all the invitations were sent off and 2.15 and Gran sat down to plan the tea for everyone afterwards.

'We could put out plates of cold meats and ham and tongue,' suggested Gran, 'and salads and that.'

'Desist, madam, I pray you,' cried 2.15.

'Why, what's wrong?' demanded Gran.

'It is cruel to eat the poor animals,' explained 2.15. 'Before they became someone's supper they had mothers and fathers who loved them.'

'But 2.15,' protested Gran, 'not so long ago you wanted to eat Lucy and me.'

'I know, I know,' groaned the wolf. 'I'm deeply ashamed – but now I have seen the light and there will be no meat at my cubs' christening.'

'What do you suggest instead then?' asked Gran, feeling a bit bewildered.

'Lots of cheese,' replied the wolf. 'And eggs and shrimps and sardines and salmon.'

'I don't see the difference between eating meat and fish,' said Gran sharply.

'But there is, there is,' insisted the wolf. 'You see until they're caught the little fishies swim around and enjoy life, which isn't true of animals. They live miserable lives until they are killed to make someone's supper.'

'All right,' said Gran, who was a bit unsure about 2.15's argument. 'It's your celebration, so I'll do it the way you want it.'

'Madam,' said 2.15, 'you are a paragon among women. But I don't want you to overwork. I'll help you with the preparations.'

'Don't worry,' replied Gran, 'Grandad will help, and Lucy. It'll be fine. You'll see we'll have a feast fit for a king.'

'What are you going to call the children?' asked Gran. 'After the time they were born, I suppose.'

'Oh no,' said 2.15 quickly. 'That would be very boring. No, their names are Romula, Remus and Mowgli.'

Gran looked surprised.

'After people who were brought up by wolves,' explained 2.15. 'Romulus and Remus, who founded Rome. Only it's Romula because one of them is a girl. And Mowgli out of *The Jungle Book*. All quite logical. Nice names, don't you think?'

'Well, yes, I suppose so,' said Gran doubtfully.

Later that day Gran told Grandad about 2.15's plans.

'I'm not happy about this christening, Bert. 3.45 is against it and 2.15's so full of funny ideas at the moment, who knows what will happen.'

'What bothers me, Mavis,' said Grandad, 'is I'm letting the 'ole village know 'e's 'ere. I mean not everyone feels the way we do about wolves.'

'I agree, Bert,' sighed Gran. 'But his heart is set on it and none of us could ever stop 2.15 when he made up his mind about something.'

When the day for the christening finally arrived Gran and Grandad and Lucy laid the tables in the village hall with heavy hearts. 2.15 had asked for each of the cubs to have a godfather and godmother and had chosen Grandad, Sir Samuel and Mr Al-u-din and Gran, Lucy and Liz Howes for the honours.

By 2 o'clock all 2.15's friends were packed into the little Norman church. The Reverend Bell was delighted to see his church so full and welcomed everyone warmly. 2.15 and the godparents clustered round the font. 3.45 lay on the floor guarding the cubs and looking very cross.

'I don't hold with christenings,' she muttered.

All went well until the moment came for the vicar to sprinkle water on Romula, the first of the cubs. As the water touched her she shrieked and bit the vicar's hand. 2.15 grabbed Romula:

'You naughty little cub,' he admonished her. 'Now you show the vicar that you're sorry.'

Romula looked unrepentant and 3.45 growled: 'Serves him right.'

'Sir,' cried 2.15, 'I must apologise for the appalling conduct of my family. Pray do not be downcast or diverted from the task in hand. I myself will hold the nose of the next two and protect you from further molestations.'

So the christening went on. Remus got his name and blessing without any mishap. Then it was Mowgli's turn. Just as the vicar was finishing, 'And I name thee Mowgli in the name of the father, son and holy ghost,' Mowgli wriggled free and fell into the font with a splash, dren-

12

ching the vicar and most of the people standing round. 2.15 quickly grabbed Mowgli and gave him to 3.45 while he helped the vicar dry himself. The congregation tried not to laugh.

'Get everyone over to the church hall, Lucy,' whispered Gran. 'The sooner this is over the better.'

So Lucy led the guests through the churchyard and into the pretty hall which was decorated with flowers and streamers. The food at the party was delicious and everyone tucked in. 2.15 walked around introducing people to each other and being an excellent host. 3.45 lay under one of the tables and watched the events with suspicion.

'How come there's no meat at this party?' demanded Pete Grubb. 'Doesn't seem like a proper party without a bit of ham or that.'

'I've become a vegetarian,' explained 2.15. 'Since I've

become a father I cannot tolerate the idea of eating some other poor animal's babies, so there it is.'

'Funny way of looking at things for a wolf,' said Pete Grubb sourly. 'And you'd better not go telling Lord Muxborough that or I'll be out of a job.'

'Who's Lord Muxborough?' asked 2.15.

'He's my boss,' explained Pete Grubb. 'He's the Lord of the Manor round here. That big house you can see from here is Muxborough Hall.'

'Ah,' said 2.15, 'so that's what it is. I've been looking at that house from my forest for hundreds of years. I was here long before that house, of course, but I've been watching the people who live there for generations. And what do you do for him?'

'I'm his lordship's gamekeeper,' replied Pete Grubb. 'And very nice work it is too.'

At that moment 2.15 noticed that Pete Grubb's leg was dangerously near 3.45's head. She was studying his ankle with a ferocious gaze.

'Come and meet my friend, Sir Samuel Wolf,' said 2.15 quickly. 'I know he is very anxious to meet you.'

'That poor fellow you kidnapped?' asked Pete Grubb. 'Yes, I'd like to meet him. I'm surprised he agreed to be a godfather to one of your children after what you did to him.'

When everyone had finished eating and chatting Gran stood on a chair and asked for quiet.

'Raise your glasses in a toast, first to the Reverend Bell, who was tolerant enough to christen three cubs, secondly to Romula, Remus and Mowgli and thirdly to the proud parents 2.15 and 3.45.'

'To the Reverend Bell, Romula, Remus, Mowgli, 2.15 and 3.45,' echoed everyone.

Gran looked down from her chair and noticed that the

14

tablecloth loaded with food, plates, glasses, cups, saucers and cutlery was being slowiy dragged to the floor.

'Stop,' she shouted. Too late, for with a huge crash the tablecloth fell to the ground, spreading food and smashed glass all round. The assembled crowd looked at the table with the three cubs sitting underneath grinning broadly.

'Just look at their faces,' said Pete Grubb. 'They did it on purpose.'

3.45 growled and Pete Grubb fell silent.

'My little ones have been just a tiny bit naughty,' said 2.15. 'I do apologise for the shock to which you have been subjected. Pray congregate on the other side of the room and continue to enjoy yourselves while I clear up.'

Lucy, Gran and Grandad helped 2.15 to clear up.

'I think you'd better get 3.45 to take the cubs home,' suggested Gran. 'They might get cut with all this broken glass.'

'All right,' agreed 3.45. 'I never wanted to get involved in all of this in the first place,' she barked.

The cubs looked at their mother and ran off to hide. 3.45 ran after them. They were obviously having a lovely time.

'Don't just stand there, 2.15,' cried Lucy. 'Do something! Those cubs are being very naughty.'

'Nonsense,' said 2.15. 'They're just full of life. Come along, my little cublings, off you go with your mother.'

The cubs took no notice until 3.45 pounced on Mowgli and picked him up in her teeth. She gave him a good shake and then handed him to 2.15:

'Look after him,' she said fiercely, 'while I get the other two.'

Mowgli bit 2.15's ear and seemed to be shouting encouragement at the other two to continue evading their mother.

'Make him stop it,' cried Lucy.

'Who's being a naughty little wolfy then?' said 2.15. 'Who's not helping Mummy get his naughty little brother and sister?'

'Honestly, 2.15,' commented Gran. 'You're hopeless. You let those cubs get away with murder.'

'They're only young once,' said 2.15, 'and I want them to enjoy it.'

'Soft,' said Grandad, 'that's what you are, soft.'

Eventually 3.45 had all three of the cubs together.

'Put them on my back,' she said. 'I'll take them home.'

The three cubs clambered on to her back.

'Wave bye bye, darlings,' cooed 2.15.

The three cubs waved and laughed as 3.45 bore them away.

'I reckon they're going to be a lot of trouble, those cubs,' said Pete Grubb, feeling much freer to express his opinions now that 3.45 had gone. 'Five wolves is too many for one village, you just wait and see.'

2

The Gamekeeper

Rather to her surprise Lucy saw quite a lot of 2.15 after the christening. Often as she walked home from school the wolf would run out and ask her to come and look at the cubs.

'Aren't they wonderful?' he would say fondly, and when Lucy had played with the cubs for a while, he would accompany her through the forest. One day he asked her:

'What is a gamekeeper anyway?'

'I'm not absolutely sure,' replied Lucy. 'I think they look after game.'

'That much is clear even to the least well informed among us, dear heart, but what exactly is game?'

'Oh, pheasants and things,' said Lucy vaguely.

'Oh, I see. So old Grubb looks after all the pheasants and things and makes sure that no one eats them?'

'Well no,' said Lucy, thinking hard, 'not exactly. The gamekeeper makes sure that the wrong people don't shoot the pheasants.'

'Oh,' mused 2.15, looking puzzled, 'I don't understand. Who are the right people?'

'Lord Muxborough and his friends. He owns the land, so he can decide who shoots the birds on it.'

'Ah,' exclaimed the wolf, 'so the gamekeeper doesn't defend the game against everybody, only against the wrong people.'

'That's it,' agreed Lucy.

'So the poor little game do get eaten in the end, but

only by the right people?'

'Well yes, something like that. Why?'

'Just wondered,' explained 2.15. 'See you soon. Byee.'

A few days later Lucy and Grandad were walking through the forest on a particularly beautiful day. Suddenly there was a rustling in the undergrowth.

'Is that you, Bert?' came a familiar voice. 'Come on over here.'

'Now 2.15,' said Grandad severely, 'you just come on out here and pack in pretendin' that you're Pete Grubb.'

'Cut it out, Bert,' came the voice. 'It *is* me, Pete Grubb.'

'Then come out of the bushes and stop messin' around.'

'I can't, someone stole my clothes when I went swimming. I can't come out. I'm only wearing my underpants.'

'Oh dear,' said Grandad, trying not to laugh. 'What do you want me to do?'

'Go to my house,' hissed Pete Grubb, 'and get my missus to bring me some clothes.'

'All right, Pete,' said Grandad. 'Don't go worrying yourself. I'll be back in a tick. Come on Lucy.'

Lucy and Grandad walked back as fast as they could along the little path that led through the forest. They walked in silence, both feeling a bit uneasy at the turn of events. When they got to the Grubb house, Grandad knocked on the door.

'Oh, hello Bert,' said Lily Grubb, 'I thought you were Pete, he's about due home.'

'Yes, well he – that is what I've called about,' muttered Grandad. 'You see, oh well it's like this. Pete went swimmin' and someone stole 'is clothes, so 'e's 'iding in the forest in 'is knickers and would like you to take 'im some clothes, quick as poss.'

'Well,' exclaimed Lily Grubb, 'there's a thing. I'll just

get some of Pete's clothes and we can be off.'

Half an hour later Grandad, Lucy, Pete and Lily Grubb were trudging through the woods back to the Grubbs' house.

'Come on in and have a cup of tea,' said Pete. 'It's the least I can do. Goodness knows how long I'd have been there if you hadn't come along.'

'Who could have done such a thing?' asked Lily Grubb as she made the tea. 'I mean, it doesn't make sense does it?'

Lucy wriggled uneasily in her seat.

'You didn't see 2.15 anywhere near, did you, Mr Grubb?' she asked.

'I didn't see anyone. One minute my clothes were there and the next moment they were gone.'

'It's very odd,' commented Grandad. 'Who would want your work clothes. I can't make any sense of it.'

Just as he made this observation there was an angry knock at the door. Pete Grubb got up to answer it. There stood Lord Muxborough, red in the face with rage.

'All right Grubb,' he shouted. 'I've just come to tell you that you're sacked. After the way you behaved this afternoon you don't need me to tell you why.'

'I don't know what you're talking about,' protested Pete Grubb. 'I don't, I honestly don't.'

'Ha,' shouted Lord Muxborough, 'a likely story. First of all you threaten to shoot me if I go anywhere near me own game and then you pretend you haven't done anything, standing there waving a gun under my nose and shouting a load of rubbish about there being no such thing as a right person when it came to shooting game and that there were only wrong people or some such piffle. You gone mad or something, Grubb?'

'No, sir, honestly it wasn't me,' moaned Pete Grubb. 'I

19

went swimming and someone stole my clothes. It was an imposter who threatened to shoot you.'

'A likely story,' snapped Lord Muxborough. 'What a load of old tommy rot! You'll have to do better than that, Grubb. I mean, for God's sake man, who would steal your old clothes? Tell me that.'

'It was that wolf,' declared Pete Grubb. 'He's got it in for me, that's why he did it.'

'Wolf!' yelled Lord Muxborough. 'Which wolf?'

'2.15,' shouted Pete Grubb, 'the wolf out of Red Riding Hood.'

Lord Muxborough stared at him in disbelief:

'You *are* mad Grubb, stark staring mad. First of all you threaten to shoot me and then you try to tell me it's some wolf out of a fairy tale. Grubb, you're sacked!'

Grandad and Lucy left Pete Grubb feeling very sorry for himself and very angry.

'I'll get my own back,' he said. 'You just watch.'

Over supper they told Lucy's Mum and Dad what had happened.

'What I want to know,' stated Grandad, 'is why Lucy is so sure that 2.15 had something to do with it?'

' 'Cos he was asking me the other day what game-keepers did and I explained to him that they protected the game against the wrong people like poachers but not against the right people like Lord Muxborough. He got quite indignant about it.'

'Oh well,' sighed Grandad, 'then it must have been him.'

'What do you think we should do?' asked Lucy. 'It's a bit hard on Mr Grubb, losing his job like that.'

They all sat silently for a while and then Lucy said:

'Grandad, you know how honest 2.15 is and the way he wants everyone to live happily ever after?'

' 'e seems to 'ave gone off all that a bit lately,' said Grandad sourly, 'losin' the poor man 'is job.'

'Well, I think he'll return Pete Grubb's clothes tonight. He wouldn't keep what wasn't his. Let's wait up for 2.15 and tell him what's happened. Maybe he'll know what to do to put it right.'

'No harm in tryin', I suppose.'

So the two of them sat up playing cards and drinking cocoa and listening hard for any sound from the forest. At about midnight Lucy heard a scuffle nearby. She ran and opened the front door.

'2.15,' she called in a loud whisper.

'Hello, dear heart,' came the wolf's voice, 'I'll be with you in a brief moment. There is just a small errand I must fulfil before I can give you my undivided attention.'

And he ran into Pete Grubb's house carrying a package and out again without it.

'Well,' said the wolf smiling broadly, 'what a nice surprise to find you both up at this late hour.'

'We were waiting for you,' said Grandad sourly.

'For me?' said 2.15 looking surprised, 'But how did you know that I would pass this way tonight?'

'Because Lucy says you're an honest kind of a wolf, and given that we know it was you that nicked poor old Grubb's gear, we thought you would bring 'em back tonight.'

'Well of course. What would I want with Pete Grubb's clothes?'

'You 'ad 'em long enough to lose the poor man 'is job,' yelled Grandad.

'Lost his job! Whatever do you mean?'

'After what you said to Lord Muxborough, poor old Pete got the blame and Lord Muxborough gave him the sack.'

21

'Oh dear,' groaned 2.15, 'that was not a part of my great scheme. I was just trying to protect the game against the right people as well as the wrong people.'

'Honestly, 2.15,' complained Lucy, 'you just go barging in without thinking. Pete Grubb knows it was you and he's very cross.'

'Yes,' chipped in Grandad, 'and I don't blame 'im. Now what are you going to do?'

'Dear friends, I pray do not look so unhappy,' cried the wolf. 'As soon as the sun is high in the sky I shall take myself off to Lord Muxborough's mansion, where I shall acquaint him with the true facts of the matter and persuade him to give Grubb his job back.'

'That'll only make matters worse,' groaned Grandad.

'Not so,' declared the wolf. 'Fear not, dear friends. In a few hours this matter will be resolved to the satisfaction of all parties. Now I must go off back to the greenwood and my little ones before 3.45 begins to worry.' And he scampered back into the forest before they could say anything more.

'Oh well,' said Grandad, 'nothing more I can do now. Better go home to Gran now. I'll see you tomorrow morning up at Muxborough Hall. One of us will 'ave to explain what all this is about and I suppose it'll be me as usual.'

The next morning Lord Muxborough came down to breakfast as usual and there, sitting quietly at the breakfast table, tucking into bacon, eggs, mushrooms, kippers, sausages, toast and tea, was 2.15.

'Good morning sir,' cried the wolf. 'As I got here before you I took the liberty of helping myself to a spot of breakfast. Take a plate for yourself and join me.'

'Well,' gasped Lord Muxborough. He flopped down

opposite 2.15 and stared with his mouth open. 2.15 finished a mouthful of egg, wiped his mouth with a napkin and then looked hard at Lord Muxborough.

'What's the matter?' asked the wolf in a concerned tone. 'Aren't you hungry?'

'Well,' said Lord Muxborough again, 'so Grubb was telling the truth after all when he went on about the wolf in Red Riding Hood.'

'Yes, of course he was. Now come on. I insist you eat some breakfast before everything gets cold. As you've had a bit of a shock I'll get it for you. Would a little of everything be in order?'

'Oh yes,' said Lord Muxborough faintly. 'Thank you very much.'

So over breakfast, 2.15 told Lord Muxborough all about Lucy and 3.45 and Gran and Grandad and Sir Samuel Wolf and how he'd had to kidnap him:

'And so the Commissioner of the London Police phoned the Queen who said that I was an old, old friend and that I should be allowed to go back to my forest with my beloved 3.45 without let or hindrance and here I am.'

'Well,' stammered Lord Muxborough, 'I never heard the like of it in all my life, damned if I have.'

At that moment Lady Muxborough came into the room and glowered at 2.15.

'Get rid of him,' she said firmly to Lord Muxborough. 'You know I don't like strangers calling in for breakfast.'

'Well yes, my dear,' replied Lord Muxborough, 'but this is a slightly exceptional case. You see Mr eh . . .'

'2.15.'

'Mr 2.15 is an old friend of the Queen's.'

'Oh,' said Lady Muxborough, her face suddenly wreathed in smiles. 'Oh well, in that case he's very welcome, very welcome indeed.'

'Thank you, dear lady,' said 2.15, and gallantly spread some marmalade on toast and handed it to her.

'And my dear, it turns out that 2.15 is also an old friend of ours, for he is none other than the wolf out of Red Riding Hood, and it seems he stole or rather borrowed Grubb's clothes yesterday. You remember the game-keeper I was telling you about?'

'Yes, dear, I remember,' said Lady Muxborough. 'Such extraordinary behaviour.'

'That was me,' said 2.15 quickly. 'I was sorry for the game and I thought they should be protected from everyone, not just the wrong people.'

'I don't follow,' said a puzzled Lady Muxborough.

2.15 explained what he had learned from Lucy and went on: 'So then I saw old Grubb taking a swim and I remembered the story of my good friend Puss in Boots who stole the Marquis's clothing while the good man was swimming, and voilà, I did the same thing. Then, dis-guised as a gamekeeper (for Madam I am a master of disguises), I met your husband and explained to him about thinking he was a right person but that he was in fact a wrong person and that the game should be allowed to live out their natural lives and not be shot just to entertain someone or fill a stew pot one night.'

'It is a bit steep, old chap,' complained Lord Muxbor-ough, 'not to be allowed to shoot me own game. I mean Muxboroughs have been shooting game on this land for hundreds of years.'

'I know that,' agreed 2.15. 'I've been watching them for hundreds of years.'

'You've been around that long?' asked Lady Muxborough.

'Oh, more,' said 2.15. 'Much more.'

'Well, I think you're a bit extreme about this game

business,' declared Lord Muxborough. 'And not entirely consistent. I noticed you wolfing down, I mean eating, that bacon not so long ago.'

'It's true,' admitted 2.15. 'What a hypocrite I am. I quite forgot, but bacon is so delicious, and I swear that from this moment not another slither of meat shall cross my lips. I owe it to other animals to be a vegetarian.'

'That's all well and good, old chap,' muttered Lord Muxborough, 'but it's not just the eating of the game, you know. I mean the shoot is a tradition, and Muxboroughs have been doing it for hundreds of years.'

'Yes, dear friend,' cried the wolf, 'but traditions can be changed. I myself have given up a time-honoured tradition of eating grannies and have even become a vegetarian. If I can do it so can you.'

'Well, to tell you the truth,' said Lady Muxborough,

'don't spread it around, but we're very hard up and we sell the game to help pay the bills.'

'That's right,' confirmed Lord Muxborough. 'Shooting game is our livelihood.'

'Don't worry about that,' said 2.15. 'I'll think of an alternative. But talking of Mr Grubb, now that you know that it was I and not him that threatened you yesterday, can we tell him that he's got his old job back?'

'I'll phone him up straight away,' agreed Lord Muxborough. 'Poor chap must be worried silly.'

'I'd be most grateful,' said 2.15, 'then my mind would be at rest and I could go back to 3.45 and my three little ones.'

So Lord Muxborough phoned Pete Grubb and told him that 2.15 had made a clean breast of things, that it had all been a mistake and that he hoped Pete Grubb would return to his job after a week's holiday on full pay.

'He says he will,' Lord Muxborough told 2.15. 'So in the end you did the fella a good turn.'

'Yes,' said the wolf smiling, 'I'm like that.'

3

The Apple Orchard

From then on 2.15 went to see the Muxboroughs regularly. One afternoon they were sitting on the terrace sipping tea when Lord Muxborough sighed a deep sigh.

'I'm going to have to sell the apple orchard for development. Breaks my heart to do it but there's no choice.'

'No choice!' repeated 2.15. 'What do you mean, no choice? There must be some other way.'

'Not one that I can see, old boy. Pity, I've always loved that orchard, particularly in the spring when the blossoms are out.'

'So have I,' agreed 2.15. 'And I refuse to let you sell the orchard. Now explain to me just why the orchard has to go.'

'Because we can't sell the apples any more,' explained Lord Muxborough. 'People don't eat as many apples as they used to. What with things like yoghourt and ice-cream, we can't sell the apples. The orchard is just there for decoration, so we either have to sell it for development or plant something sensible like potatoes that don't look pretty.'

'Are you really that hard up?' demanded the wolf.

'Well yes, old chap. I mean you don't want me to sell the game, and the house needs a new roof and the carpets inside are falling to bits. The running of these big old houses costs an arm and a leg. Just can't keep it up any more.'

'What do other dukes and lords and people with big houses do?'

'They open 'em up the public,' replied Lord Muxborough.

'Then why don't you do that?'

'Because there are too many stately homes open to the public,' said Lord Muxborough. 'There's nothing special about Muxborough Hall. No one would bother to come here.'

'What's so special about the ones people do bother to go to?' asked 2.15.

'Oh, some have a safari park or a car museum or a fun park,' replied Lord Muxborough, 'but Lady M wouldn't have them. And anyway, I don't have any money to get anything installed.'

'Umm,' said the wolf thoughtfully. 'What else could you provide that might be a bit less intrusive?'

'We don't have a resident ghost or anything like that.'

'I have it,' cried 2.15. 'Does any other stately home have a resident wolf?'

'Well, eh no, not that I know of.'

'Well then, I shall become your wolf guide. After all, I've lived round here for hundreds of years, and I remember the Muxboroughs better than anyone. I shall accompany the tourists around and explain the history of the house and the area and then pose for pictures for an extra 50p and all the proceeds will go to the upkeep of the house, but only if you promise faithfully not to sell the orchard.'

'Terribly nice of you, old boy, most grateful,' said Lord Muxborough. 'Have to chat to Lady M about it but I think it sounds like a damned good idea. But why are you so concerned about that orchard?'

'It's because of my little ones,' explained the wolf. 'I

want them to get as much pleasure out of looking at that orchard as I always have. Wouldn't want them to have to look at lots of boring old houses or a car park or something. So it's not just a question of you and Lady M living happily ever after, though of course I most cordially hope that you do, but of preserving the countryside for my babies.'

'How do you think you'd feel about being a guide several times a day?' asked Lord Muxborough.

'I expect I'll find it very tedious but it is necessary. And talking of that, I think it might be a good idea if you were to take me to one or two of the stately homes that are currently open to the public and let me see what goes on there for myself.'

'Steady on, old chap,' said Lord Muxborough, 'don't you think people might be just a touch alarmed to see a wolf prancing through a stately home?'

'I'll pretend I'm your dog,' explained 2.15 patiently, 'it's what I usually do when I'm among people.'

'Well, to be perfectly honest with you old chap, I don't think that would help all that much. I mean they aren't too keen on strange dogs in stately homes either.'

'Don't tell me NO DOGS ALLOWED,' groaned the wolf. 'It's a scandal!'

'I'm sure you're right, old chap,' muttered Lord Muxborough, 'that there are perfectly well-behaved dogs up and down the country just desperate to see a stately home. But that's just the way it is. So where do we go from here?'

'No problem,' cried 2.15. 'Surely you must be well acquainted with many of the owners of these stately homes. At least some must be your tried and trusted friends.'

'Well, yes,' agreed Lord Muxborough. 'There's old

Pongo, Duke of Bentford; went to school with him. Then there's Foxy Fairhead-ffoulkes; travel up to the House of Lords with him. And then of course there's dear old Diana, Duchess of Cornshire; always had a soft spot for Diana, what!'

'Well then,' said 2.15, 'another obstacle overcome. Now, sir, you must ring up one of these old friends and ask to visit them.' Say you are thinking of opening up Muxborough Hall to the public and want to learn from them. You take me along as your trusted hound and together we will learn the art of stately home management.'

'Dashed good plan,' beamed Lord Muxborough. 'Got to say it, 2.15, you're a damned clever chap. Never too strong in the brains department myself, appreciate your help. We'll start off by going to see old Pongo, if that's all right with you?'

Within a few days Lord Muxborough and 2.15 were ready to set off in Lord Muxborough's Land Rover to go visiting. Lady Muxborough was standing in the drive waiting to wave them goodbye.

Suddenly there was a noise from the orchard and out pranced 3.45 with Romula, Remus and Mowgli in tow.

'Ah,' cried 2.15, leaping from the vehicle, 'my children have come to bid me a fond farewell and my loving wife also.'

'I have not,' snapped 3.45. 'I've come to find out what all this is about. I'm not having you go off whenever you feel like it and leaving the children. You've got responsibilities now.'

'My love, my love, it's just because of those responsibilities that I must undertake this trip.'

31

'Huh!' growled 3.45, sounding unconvinced. 'It's just you and your helping-people-to-live-happily-ever-after kick again.'

'No, dearest, truly it isn't,' replied 2.15. 'If I don't help Lord Muxborough, he'll have to cut down the orchard. Now I want my children and their children's children to have the privilege of enjoying this forest and its surrounds as beautiful and unspoiled as it is today.'

'So why do you have to go with him?' demanded 3.45. 'Just tell him that if he cuts down the orchard I'll eat him up and he won't do it. No need to go gallivanting off again.'

'Don't go, Daddy, don't go,' chorused the cubs, and they jumped up at the car and began to scratch the paintwork. 'Don't go, Daddy, let Mummy eat the man all up.'

Lord and Lady Muxborough clung together terrified.

'Quiet, children, quiet,' said 2.15. '3.45, look what you've done. You've scared my good friends Lord and Lady Muxborough. Dear sir and madam, pray do not be alarmed. This is my sweet wife, 3.45, and her bark is much worse than her bite.'

'He's a liar,' growled 3.45. 'My bite is a lot worse than my bark and I feel like proving it this very moment.'

'Desist!' cried 2.15.

'Go on, Mummy!' yelled the three cubs. 'Go on, bite him, bite them both.'

'This will have to stop,' declared 2.15. 'My love, you are setting a very bad example to the children. Now I am going off with Lord Muxborough, but we will be back before nightfall, and then I shall stay home with you and the children for ever more.'

'Well, all right,' growled 3.45, 'if it really is just this once.'

'Of course it's just this once,' smiled 2.15, giving her a kiss. 'Who would want to leave such a sweet wife and such lovely children?'

'Can we go with Daddy?' shrieked Remus.

'I want to go in a car,' yelled Mowgli.

'I want to scare people,' squeaked Romula falling into the driver's seat.

'Aren't they sweet?' said 2.15 smiling indulgently. 'Now come along cubs, we'd love to take you with us but it's not practical this time. You stay with Mummy and next time Lord Muxborough will let you come.'

'All right,' snapped 3.45. 'We'll let you go but you see you're back by nightfall – or else.'

'Farewell, my darlings,' called 2.15 as 3.45 stomped off back into the forest followed by the three rollicking cubs. 'Be good little ones. Do just what Mummy tells you.'

Lord Muxborough mopped his brow.

'That was a close run thing,' he said as he staggered into his car.

'Not so, dear friend,' 2.15 reassured him, 'nothing to worry about. It's just that 3.45 was in the zoo and is a tiny bit cross with people.'

So 2.15 and Lord Muxborough drove off. When they arrived at the Duke of Bentford's magnificent sixteenth century house, the Duke wanted to show Lord Muxborough around on their own.

'Dashed nice of you to offer, Pongo, old chap,' said Lord Muxborough cheerfully. 'That would be simply splendid.'

2.15 growled and nudged Lord Muxborough with his head. Lord Muxborough knelt down:

'All right boy, what is it?'

'We don't want a special tour,' whispered 2.15 in his ear. 'We want to go round with the tourists and see what it's like. Find an excuse to change your mind.'

'Eh, Pongo old boy,' stammered Lord Muxborough, 'just had a thought. It wouldn't really be much help being shown round by you, need to see what it's like for the general public really – you know the sort of thing.'

'Well, if that's what you want, Muffy, it's up to you. Like to leave yer hound with me?'

'No, I'll take him with me, if you don't mind, Pongo old boy. He doesn't like being left with strangers. Get's a bit snappish, so if it's all the same to you I'll take him along.'

So the Duke of Bentford explained to the guide that Lord Muxborough was a friend of his and that it would be all right for him to take his dog on the tour. 2.15 trotted along behind Lord Muxborough and listened to all the details of how the house had been begun in the reign of Henry VIII by the first Duke and expanded ever since. He looked at the bed Queen Elizabeth I had slept in,

walked along corridors full of portraits of the Dukes of
Bentford, saw the picture of the wife of the fifth Duke
who disappeared in mysterious circumstances and was
reputed to haunt the house. Then he looked intently at
the bedrooms, the kitchen, the ballroom and the huge
staircase and then followed the others into the café. The
Duke of Bentford came up and invited Lord Muxborough
to tea in the house.

'Thanks, Pongo old boy,' said Lord Muxborough
gratefully. 'Tiring tour. I don't mind if I do.'

2.15 growled and scratched Lord Muxborough with his
paw. Lord Muxborough looked down and 2.15 shook his
head vehemently:

'Oh, Pongo old chap,' muttered Lord Muxborough,
'forgot for a moment why I was here. Ought to go and see
what the provisions are for the public, don't you know. I'll
just go and have a look to see what you provide in the way

of refreshments and then have a quick nose round the
jolly old souvenir shop and then 2.15 and I will join you
upstairs.'

'2.15?' said the Duke, looking bewildered.

'Name of me dog,' explained Lord Muxborough.

'Funny name,' commented the Duke.

'Suppose so,' agreed Lord Muxborough and disappeared in the direction of the tea rooms.

They had tea and then Lord Muxborough led 2.15
round the souvenir shop. When no one was looking Lord
Muxborough bent down and whispered in 2.15's ear:

'Anything else you want to see, old chap?'

'I've seen what I need,' whispered 2.15. 'Let's go.'

So they went upstairs to the Duke of Bentford's drawing room and 2.15 dutifully lay at Lord Muxborough's
feet.

'Ready for a spot of tea?' suggested the Duke. 'Tea,
sandwiches and a few cakes, if that's all right with you,
Muffy, and some water and biscuits for your dog? That
sound all right to you?'

'Splendid, Pongo old boy, that would just about hit the
spot.'

'It most certainly would not,' interrupted 2.15, in an
aggrieved tone. 'I'll thank you, Duke, to order tea,
sandwiches and cakes for three, and no messing about
with dog biscuits.'

'Well!' said the Duke of Bentford, sitting down in the
nearest chair and staring hard at 2.15. 'Well I'll be blowed
if the hound didn't talk.'

'Good afternoon, sir,' said 2.15 holding out a paw.
'Please don't be alarmed. My name is 2.15 and I am the
wolf out of Red Riding Hood. No doubt you read about
me when you were a little lad.'

'Well, yes, but I didn't think you were real.'

'Don't let that concern you,' replied 2.15. 'You are not alone in that assumption, but the fact is that for hundreds of years I've been living in the forest near Lord Muxborough's estate. But what is more important at the moment is that I have very refined tastes and do not relish the thought of imbibing water and biscuits for my tea. So I'll join you and Muffy here for tea.'

'Pleasure,' said the Duke. 'Not every day do I get the chance to have tea with a talking wolf.'

So over tea 2.15 and Lord Muxborough told the Duke of Bentford everything about the orchard and all the problems that Muxborough Hall were having.

'Well, I think all your problems are behind you now, Muffy old boy,' exclaimed the Duke. 'With a guide like 2.15 you'll have them pouring in. You'll make an absolute fortune.'

'Sir, I hope from the bottom of my heart that your optimistic predictions are right, but now we must go, for if I'm not home soon, 3.45 will be very cross, and I like to be home in time for the little ones' bath time.'

'Bye, Pongo old boy,' called Lord Muxborough as he drove away.

'Bye, Muffy and 2.15, and good luck with your venture.'

On the way back 2.15 suddenly burst out:

'I've got the most brilliant idea.'

'Jolly good,' said Lord Muxborough, 'let's hear it.'

'All the apples in the orchard that you can't sell, we'll get Gran and Grandad to start making things from them and we can sell them. You could have apple pie, apple tart, apple crumble, apple turnover, apple snow, apple charlotte, toffee apples for the children, apple this and apple that, and then you could sell them to the tourists.'

'That's a dashed good idea,' agreed Lord Muxborough.

'This whole thing begins to seem more and more likely to succeed. I have to hand it to you, 2.15, you're a dashed clever chap, I mean wolf.'

'I am, aren't I?' said 2.15, smiling immodestly. 'And if you employ Grubb as ticket collector everyone will be well taken care of.'

4

The Tour Guide

That evening 2.15 rushed round to see Gran and Gran-dad.

'I had the most wonderful idea,' he said.

'Oh yeh,' said Grandad. 'So what 'ave you achieved with all your capering round the stately 'omes of England?'

'You and Gran are going to run the Apple Parlour to use up the apples in the orchard and give yourselves some extra income to supplement your meagre pension.'

'What are you on about, 2.15?' demanded Grandad. 'You're not makin' any sense.'

'Lord Muxborough is opening up the old hall to tourists. I will be the tour guide and chief attraction and there will be a need for somewhere for the good tourists to partake of some nourishment. That is where you come in. You and Gran will make apple pies, and apple tarts and apple snow and apple dumplings and apple charlotte and apple turnovers and sell them for gain.'

'You must be barmy,' snapped Grandad. 'If you think I'm goin' to slave my fingers to the bone to help some lord, you're wrong.'

'But you need the money,' 2.15 pointed out. 'You yourself said you could hardly manage to pay all the bills on the cottage.'

'I don't want to talk about it no more,' said Grandad firmly. 'I'm not going to work for the aristocracy and that's that.'

'You've completely spoiled my little plan,' complained 2.15. 'And I'd worked it all out so beautifully.'

'It sounds like a lovely idea to me,' Gran comforted him. 'I'll do it, even if old misery here doesn't want to.'

'Well, you're the really crucial person,' 2.15 told her. 'You see, I envisage you selling all the apple things by the score, and I would pose for pictures with you and underneath would be a notice saying, "Until I tried her cakes I wanted to eat *her*", and then everyone will buy quantities.'

'Well,' said Gran, 'I'm game.'

'No you're not,' said 2.15 grinning. 'You're Gran.'

So the next morning they went up to Muxborough Hall. While they were discussing the Apple Parlour, they heard a clap of thunder.

'It's going to rain,' cried Lady Muxborough. 'Grab those pails and follow me.'

They all rushed upstairs and began to distribute the pails under the leaking roof.

'It's no good,' sighed Lady Muxborough. 'What we really need is a new roof.'

'And you shall have it, my dear,' promised Lord Muxborough. 'It's the first thing we'll do with the takings from 2.15's plan.'

'You can't wait that long,' declared Gran. 'That roof needs to be patched up temporarily or it will fall in and I know just the man to do it for you. Could I use your phone for a minute?'

Gran picked up the phone:

'Is that you, Bert Wood? Put on your skates and get over here to Muxborough Hall and bring your tool case. Don't argue with me, Bert, just get up here.'

Soon a disgruntled Grandad was standing in the middle of Muxborough Hall.

' 'ow the other 'arf lives,' he said sourly. 'It's all right for some.'

'Now you stop that, Bert,' said Gran. 'Lord and Lady Muxborough's roof is leaking something terrible.'

'Shocking business, old boy,' said Lord Muxborough. 'Haven't got a bean to my name. Try to keep the old house up but it's not easy.'

'You could get a job like everyone else,' said Grandad sourly.

'Wish I could,' agreed Lord Muxborough, 'but I never learned anything. Feel a bit sad about that, to be perfectly honest with you.'

'There you are,' said 2.15, 'the Muxboroughs are as hard up as you are so you should all set up the Apple Parlour and make a bit of money.'

'Even if I agree to do that, I don't see why I need my flippin' tools to cook some apple pies.'

'Eh no, the tools are not for that,' said 2.15. 'But we would like you to show Lord Muxborough how to mend the roof.'

'No problem there,' said Grandad. 'I'm good at roofs. Always used to fix me own. As soon as the rain stops I'll fix it for you.'

'Terrible nice of you, Mr Wood.'

'Call me Bert.'

'Muffy's the name, and this is my wife, Caroline.'

'Right you are,' said Grandad. 'Now I think that rain's stoppin' a bit. Come on, Muffy, let's go and 'ave a look at that roof of yours. You come up with me and 'and me me things as I need them and I'll show you how to mend a roof.'

'Well,' said 2.15, 'I foresee no problem now in the construction and running of the Apple Parlour.'

'Oh, well done, 2.15!' said Lady Muxborough. 'I do

41

think you are most frightfully clever. Now come on, Mavis, let's put our heads together and find some really good apple recipes.'

'Ladies,' said the wolf bowing gallantly, 'since you seem more than able to take care of these matters, I will away to my fair 3.45.' And he ran off into the forest laughing with delight.

While Grandad and Lord Muxborough constructed the Apple Parlour out of the old kitchens, 2.15 began to read up on the history of Muxborough Hall and the village of Muxborough-on-the-Marsh.

'You know,' he told Lady Muxborough, 'the history of the area really is quite fascinating. Now how would it be if we offered the tourists two alternative tours? One of Muxborough Hall alone and one of the village. That way after a walk round the village the people would be hungrier and more likely to purchase the delicious fare at the Apple Parlour.'

'It sounds like a splendid idea. Of course the people in the village would have to agree but I can't see why they wouldn't.'

'Good,' said the wolf. 'In that case I shall take a stroll through the village this afternoon and track down some spots that express the true character of the village and then I shall make a route map.'

Later that afternoon Lord Muxborough was dismayed to see 2.15 trot out of the forest with the triplets skipping along in his wake.

'You're never taking them into the village with you?' he gasped.

'I most certainly am,' replied the wolf smiling. '3.45 wants a break and I feel it is time I introduced my little ones to the big wide world. Say hello to Lord Muxborough, little ones.'

'Good afternoon, Lord Muck,' chorused the triplets giggling. 2.15 smiled indulgently.

'They don't mean it, Muffy. It's just that they still have problems with long words.'

'Well, keep a sharp eye on them, 2.15,' he advised. 'Have a nice afternoon.'

As they disappeared out of sight, Lord Muxborough told his wife:

'Silly chap's taken those terrible triplets into the village with him.'

'Oh dear,' said Lady Muxborough. 'That sounds like a recipe for disaster.'

'Quite so,' agreed her husband. 'Thought of offering to look after them meself, but thought better of it.'

'Very sensible, Muffy,' said Lady Caroline. 'They're such a handful, those three. We don't need them around Muxborough Hall.'

As they reached Muxborough-on-the-Marsh, 2.15 and his troop walked past Gran and Grandad's cottage.

' 'ere comes 2.15,' Grandad told Gran. 'Cor blimey, I don't believe 'e's got those dreadful cubs in tow.'

'Come away from the window, Bert,' said Gran quickly. 'Best pretend we're out. We don't want to hurt 2.15's feelings but I don't want those three tearaways in here.'

So Gran and Grandad crouched down while the procession of wolves went past. Gran got up and peeped round the curtain:

'They're going into the village,' she whispered.

'Oh dear, oh lor, there'll be some mischief done today.'

2.15 however continued blithely on his way:

'All right, my little ones,' he told the triplets. 'This is our local village of Muxborough-on-the-Marsh and

Daddy is going to take you on a little walk around. Now, are you all going to be good?'

'Oh yes, Daddy,' chorused the cubs. 'We're going to be very, very good.'

'Of course you are,' beamed 2.15. 'Now, little ones, this is the village shop. Come in and maybe Daddy will buy you some sweets.'

As the wolves entered the shop, the customers scattered and rushed to hide wherever they could. 2.15 looked at the scene of confusion with amazement:

'Fear not, good people,' he declaimed. 'It is I, the wolf from Red Riding Hood. For many centuries I have dwelled in the forest over yonder. I am going to be the guide at Muxborough Hall which is to be developed as a tourist attraction. So let us all be friends, and co-operate in bringing prosperity to Muxborough-on-the-Marsh.'

'You can talk,' said the shopkeeper, raising his head an inch above the counter.

'Of course I can talk,' replied 2.15 with dignity. 'You've heard the story, you know the wolf carries on conversations. After all, how could I have said, "All the better for seeing you with, etc," if I hadn't been able to speak. I want you to tell me if you would be willing to stock some cards of the village to sell to tourists if I bring them on a tour of the village?'

'Well,' said the shopkeeper standing up and looking hard at 2.15. 'I heard as how Lord Muxborough was going to open up the house and now that you mention it he did say something about a wolf, but I thought I'd heard wrong.'

One of the customers came out of a corner:

'You had a christening,' she said. 'I heard all about it but I thought the vicar was pulling my leg.'

'Not at all, madam, that auspicious occasion was to give

my little ones here names. Tell the lady what you are called, my little cublings.'

'I'm Romula.'

'I'm Remus.'

'And I'm Mowgli.'

'Oh aren't they lovely, and they can talk too.'

'Of course,' replied 2.15. 'For they are the most intelligent cubs in the world. Now sir, will you agree to stock the cards?'

'No problem there, it will be good for business.'

'Thank you, I knew I could rely on your good sense. Now my three little ones want some sweeties, don't you?'

'Oh, yes please, Daddy,' chorused the cubs.

'And what would you like?' asked the shopkeeper smiling at them.

'One of those,' said Remus, pointing to a picture of an ice-cream.

'With pleasure,' said the shopkeeper and gave him a large cone.

'I would like one of those,' squeaked Mowgli, pointing to a gobstopper.

'Then one of those you shall have.'

'And you, Romula?' asked 2.15. 'What will you have?'

There was no reply. 2.15 looked around. No Romula.

'Romula, where are you?' he called. 'Tell Daddy where you are.'

'Here,' came a muffled reply. 'I'm in here.'

'Oh, my lord,' said the shopkeeper. 'She's in the ice-cream freezer.'

He rushed over and wrenched it open and there on top of all the ice-cream sat Romula.

'Come on in,' she said enthusiastically to her brothers. 'It's lovely and cold in here.'

2.15 grabbed her and closed the lid again.

45

'You are a very naughty little cub,' he said. 'And for that you won't get a treat like your brothers.'

A tear ran down Romula's nose.

'Oh, all right,' groaned 2.15. 'Choose what you want.'

'I want to go back in there,' Romula insisted. 'And I want the boys to come with me.'

'No,' said 2.15, 'you can't.'

The three cubs all began to shriek. 2.15 grabbed them and began to back out of the door.

'I'll call you about the cards,' he said, and disappeared.

They trooped on through the village till they came to the pub. It was just closing after lunch. A few villagers were sitting outside drinking and looked up in amazement as the troop passed *The Dog and Duck* in single file, Remus licking his ice-cream and Mowgli his gobstopper.

'Goodday, gentlemen,' said 2.15. 'Lovely day for the time of year.'

'Good afternoon,' chorused the cubs.

Romula stopped.

'I'm thirsty, Daddy,' she announced. 'Look, someone has left his drink on the ground.'

And she stuck her nose in the pint of beer and lapped it up.

'It's nice,' she told her brothers. 'You should try.'

2.15 grabbed at them. He put one under each arm and held Romula kicking and giggling between his paws.

The publican came running out:

'What's going on out here?' he demanded.

When he saw 2.15 he stopped and gawped in amazement.

'He can talk, too,' the late drinkers informed him.

'Yes sir, that is quite correct,' 2.15 told him. 'I was just passing through to tell you that I am going to be the guide at Muxborough Hall and was planning to bring people on

47

a village tour. I thought you might be interested in a bit of extra business.'

'Well, I would,' stammered the landlord. 'But who are you?'

'I am 2.15, the wolf from Red Riding Hood, but nothing to worry about. I'm quite tame and living peacefully in the forest with my dear wife and my triplets.'

'One of them scoffed my drink,' complained a customer.

'That was me,' shrieked Romula, wriggling to escape from her father's grip.

'I'll be in touch about the tourists,' said 2.15 quickly and escaped up the street as fast as he could. When they reached the edge of the village he sat down and let the cubs go while he wiped his brow.

'You naughty little cubs,' he admonished them. 'Now you just play quietly while Daddy gets his breath back. Don't go far and don't bother anyone.'

'We won't,' the cubs assured him, 'we won't trouble a single soul.'

'Oh dear,' said 2.15 to himself, 'that wasn't a very good start. Maybe I should have listened to 3.45 and waited a bit longer before introducing the cubs to the world.'

Just then he heard a woman shriek and then he saw Lily Grubb running towards him.

'My washing,' she gasped, 'it's running away.'

'I'll get it back for you,' said 2.15 quickly. 'It's my cubs. They don't mean any harm. They just don't know about people and didn't realise it was washing.'

2.15 found the cubs playing with the washing with their muddy paws.

'I thought I told you not to bother anyone,' he told them sternly.

The three cubs looked up at him with wounded expressions.

'But, Daddy,' they said, 'we didn't bother anyone. We saw these things flapping in the wind and we thought they were for playing.'

2.15 took the washing from them.

'I'm so sorry,' he said to Lily Grubb. 'Can I do the washing for you? I do apologise, madam, from the bottom of my heart. No harm intended.'

'Well, I'll overlook it this time,' said Lily Grubb grudgingly, 'but you must find a way of keeping them under better control, 2.15. They're a menace.'

2.15 made his escape and returned the cubs to 3.45 and went off to report back to Lord Muxborough. He was just telling him about the helpful attitude of the publican when he heard the sound of chanting.

'Whatever is that?' said Lord Muxborough.

'Sounds like a demonstration to me,' said Grandad. 'You know, people marchin' and shoutin'.'

'Damn it, Bert, I do believe you're right, Bert,' said Lord Muxborough. 'What are they chanting?'

'Wolves out,' said 2.15 quietly, and a moment later they saw a procession marching towards Muxborough Hall carrying banners and placards. In front was Pete Grubb carrying a placard saying KEEP MUXBOROUGH-ON-THE-MARSH WOLF FREE and behind him others carried banners saying SAY NO TO WOLVES and WOLVES OUT. Behind them marched most of the population of the village.

'Don't worry about this, 2.15,' said Lord Muxborough. 'Leave it all to me.' As the marchers got near to the house the chanting subsided.

'All right, Grubb, what's all this about?' demanded Lord Muxborough.

'We're not happy about having all those wolves living near the village,' declared Pete Grubb. 'And we've got a petition signed by most of the villagers to say so.'

'Now you lot, listen to me,' shouted Lord Muxborough. 'We're very fortunate to have 2.15 and his family living here. It's what makes this village different from any other in the whole world. Out of all the villages in the world that the wolf from Red Riding Hood could have chosen, he picked ours. It's a great honour. Also he is committed to helping people live happily ever after. I myself have benefitted from his good feelings. I shall no longer have to sell my lovely orchard or close down Muxborough Hall and the only reason I can do this is because, thanks to 2.15, Muxborough-on-the-Marsh is going to be put on the map. Far from protesting against him you should be getting up a petition begging him never to leave. This village needs tourism and the money and jobs it will bring.'

'You didn't explain all of that, Pete,' said one marcher.

'No, nor about the extra jobs,' said another.

'Nor that he was the wolf out of Red Riding Hood,' said another. 'It's a privilege to have him here, he's a world famous celebrity.'

'Well,' muttered Pete Grubb, 'I hadn't exactly looked at it like that.'

The crowd were packing up their banners and beginning to move away.

'Good,' said Lord Muxborough. 'Well that's settled, then. Hey you, Grubb, don't go skulking off like that. You come here and apologise to 2.15 for organising that disgraceful exhibition of spiteful prejudice.'

'Sorry,' muttered Pete Grubb, 'but, your lordship, he does persecute me, and his cubs messed up all my wife's washing.'

'They did,' admitted 2.15, 'I do apologise.'

'Yeh, well,' said Pete Grubb, 'I'll let bygones be bygones if you will.'

'Good,' said Lord Muxborough. 'Now all we have to do is wait for the first tourists to arrive, and in the meantime, 2.15, I suggest you keep those three rascals of yours out of the village.'

5

The Harvest Festival

As soon as Muxborough Hall was opened, people poured in to see 2.15. By the end of the summer Lord Muxborough had enough money to mend the roof and 2.15 had brought so much prosperity to the village he had become a very popular figure. In the forest autumn was approaching and the apples in Lord Muxborough's orchard were being picked and stacked in large baskets. 2.15 insisted on helping and 3.45 brought the triplets to watch. After a while they got a bit bored and began wandering around the orchard and jumping up at people.

'I say, 2.15,' said Lady Muxborough, 'do you really think this is the best place for the triplets? If they go on like this someone may fall on them.'

'They don't mean any harm,' explained 2.15. 'It's just that they have such healthy high spirits. Cubs are like that.'

'Yes, I'm sure that's true,' said Lady Muxborough, 'but they could hurt someone and themselves. I really do think you should ask 3.45 to take them home.'

2.15 looked at the three cubs who were all leaping up at Pete Grubb's trouser leg and at Pete Grubb holding onto the ladder with one hand and trying to kick the cubs away with his foot. 3.45 was growling menacingly.

'I see what you mean,' said 2.15 quickly. 'All right cubs, time to go home with Mummy. Come along, darlings, you've all been very good but it is time to go now.'

'Shan't!' shouted the cubs. 'We don't want to go home, we're having fun.' And they ran round the orchard hiding behind baskets and trees.

'Get them,' yelled Pete Grubb, falling off his ladder with enthusiasm. 'Those three are a menace. Get 'em.'

Soon everyone was chasing the three cubs who loved every minute of it.

'You won't catch me,' yelled Romula, throwing an apple at Pete Grubb. It hit him on the nose.

'Or me,' squeaked Remus, throwing an apple at Lady Muxborough and knocking her glasses off.

'I'm the king of the castle,' called Mowgli, standing on a pile of baskets stacked one on top of the other. But the baskets crashed to the ground with Mowgli trapped underneath.

'My baby,' yelled 3.45, 'what have you done to my baby? Keep away, everyone, anyone who comes near gets a good bite.'

So while the pickers stood round looking anxious, 2.15 and 3.45 searched among the apples for Mowgli. Eventually they found him.

'My poor baby, are you all right?'

'Hello Mummy,' said Mowgli. 'That was fun. Can I do it again? You pile up the baskets and then we can all have a go.'

'Oh please, Mummy,' chorused Romula and Remus. 'Please let us.'

'No!' said 2.15 sternly. 'You've had plenty of fun, now it's time to go home.'

'It's not fair,' shrieked Romula and Remus. 'Mowgli had a go and we didn't, it's not fair,' and they began to cry loudly.

'Those cubs are so spoiled,' muttered Grandad. 'They get away with murder. I'd like to be in charge of them for a day or two. I'd soon change their tune.'

'Now Romula and Remus,' said 2.15 patiently, 'life's like that. It just isn't fair and sometimes we have to accept that and try not to make a fuss and . . .'

'I want to go under the basket,' wailed Romula.

'I won't go home till I have a go,' shrieked Remus.

'That's enough!' growled 3.45. 'Now come on, 2.15, you take Mowgli, I'll grab Romula and Remus, and not another squeak out of any of you, or else!'

3.45 sounded so fierce that 2.15 and the cubs did as she said and quietly left the orchard and trooped off into the forest.

The next Sunday was the Harvest Festival. The whole village packed into the old Norman church. In front of the altar were huge piles of flowers and fruit and vegetables from the surrounding farms. The Reverend Bell looked at the packed pews and smiled with delight. Gran and Grandad, Lucy and her parents had arrived a bit late and were sitting in the back. Just as the congregation had risen to sing 'We Plough the Fields and Scatter' the door of the church was flung open and in walked 2.15, 3.45 and the triplets.

'Oh no,' groaned Lucy.

'You'd think 'e'd 'ave the sense to keep them away from the 'arvest festival,' moaned Grandad.

The wolves slipped into a back pew, picked up hymn books and started to sing. When the singing was over the vicar climbed into the pulpit.

'May I welcome you all to the Parish Church of St Bede's on the Hill and say how delighted I am to welcome so many new faces, and not only people but indeed some members of the furry fraternity, and may I say that, like St Francis of Assisi, I am delighted to see them participat-

ing in Christian . . . ahhh . . .' and the vicar disappeared
from view. Lord and Lady Muxborough ran forward from
the front pew and helped the vicar up.

'Are you all right?' demanded Lady Muxborough,
brushing down the vicar's cassock.

'So sorry,' stammered the vicar, 'I feel such a fool, in
front of everyone like that, but it felt as though something
bit my ankle and as though my cassock was being pulled.'

Lady Muxborough looked round sharply, just in time to
see the triplets running into the harvest display giggling to
themselves.

'Sorry for the delay, everyone,' said Lady Muxborough, 'the service will continue in a moment. 2.15 and 3.45 would you come forward.'

2.15 pranced up. 'Is the poor man quite recovered?' he asked.

'Yes,' said Lady Muxborough sternly, 'but it was the triplets' fault. Now they're under the harvest produce. Could you persuade them to come out so that we can proceed with the service.'

'Come along, you naughty little cubs, come out and apologise to the vicar,' said 2.15.

'Shan't,' called the cubs. Potatoes began to roll down the aisle.

'My potato can roll further than yours,' yelled Romula.

'No it can't,' shrieked Remus. 'I'll make mine hit the door.'

'Romula, Remus, Mowgli,' snapped 3.45, 'You stop that and come here.'

'Come on, little ones, do what Mummy says,' coaxed 2.15.

'If you aren't out here by the time I count to five,' said 3.45 menacingly, 'you'll get no supper tonight. One, two, three, four, five.'

By the time she had finished counting, the three cubs had clambered out of the produce and were standing in a demure line next to their mother.

'Are you sure you're all right?' 3.45 asked the vicar.

'Oh yes, quite all right,' he said quickly. 'Please don't concern yourself on my behalf.'

'I won't,' 3.45 assured him. 'Come on, cubs, back to the forest and let the people get on with their service.'

'Lovely that you came,' the vicar called after the departing wolves. 'Come again any time you want.'

The next day 2.15 turned up for work at Muxborough Hall as usual.

'Sorry about the little diversion at church yesterday. My little ones are just the tiniest bit naughty sometimes, but they don't mean any harm, they're darlings really.'

'That's as maybe, 2.15,' said Lady Muxborough severely, 'but you must get them under control and not leave it all to 3.45. It's not fair on the triplets and it's not fair to the people who live here.'

'Oh dear,' sighed 2.15, 'it's just that I waited so long to be a father and I don't want to keep on saying "no" to them. I want them to feel free and enjoy life.'

'Yes, but everyone must learn to observe certain limits. And that includes wolves. Now next Saturday the village is playing cricket against a team from the next village, just for fun as the cricket season is over. Now of course you will be welcome but only if you can guarantee the behaviour of the cubs.'

'Of course we'll come,' said 2.15. 'I myself will oversee their conduct and see to it that they behave like cuddly little cherubs.'

So the next Saturday the whole village turned up on the village green. Everyone came carrying hampers full of good food. The sun was shining and there was just a hint of a breeze. 2.15 arrived with 3.45 and the triplets, and he wandered over to Gran and Lucy.

'Goodday, dear friends,' he called, 'I have brought the family to the picnic and they're on their best behaviour, aren't you, little ones?'

'Yes, Daddy,' chorused the cubs smiling demurely. 'Good afternoon, Gran and Grandad and Auntie Lucy.'

Grandad and Lucy looked rather surprised but Gran smiled and said, 'Hello 2.15 and 3.45, good afternoon triplets.'

Grandad scowled. ' 'ere,' he said gruffly, 'what's goin' on? Them triplets is plannin' something no good and I

57

want to know what it is.'

Romula sat down next to Grandad:

'Oh no, Grandpa Bert. We're all going to be very good. Daddy gave us a talking to and we all see that we've been very naughty and we're going to behave.'

'We're never ever going to be naughty again,' joined in Mowgli and Remus.

'Well, I don't believe it!' sniffed Grandad.

'Be quiet, Bert,' snapped Gran. 'Here are the triplets turning over a new leaf and all you can do is make nasty comments.'

'I bet I'm right,' said Grandad. 'By the end of today you'll 'ave to say, "I doubted you Bert, but you was right as usual".'

Gran ignored Grandad.

'Now what would you little wolves like to eat?' she asked.

'We've got ham sandwiches or beef sandwiches.'

'Neither, thank you, Gran,' said Remus politely.

'We're vegetarians you see,' explained Mowgli.

'But if you had something that did not contain meat and could spare it we would be most grateful,' piped up Romula.

2.15 beamed proudly. 'You see, my little cublets really do have the most beautiful manners.'

Gran gave the cubs a piece of cake each and they sat on the blanket and ate it very carefully, taking great care not to spill any crumbs.

'Thank you very much, Gran and Grandpa Bert, for our cake,' they chorused. 'That was very nice.'

3.45 growled, 'That man is coming towards us.'

They all looked up and saw the vicar making his way across the grass. The three cubs got up and stood in a row.

'Good afternoon,' said the Reverend Bell gaily. 'And

how are we on this lovely afternoon?'

'We're very well, thank you, Reverend Bell,' said the triplets, 'and we want to say we're sorry for being naughty at the Harvest Festival and can we please help in the Church sometimes and come to Sunday school?'

'Well!' exclaimed the Reverend Bell, 'isn't that nice. Yes little ones, I'd love to see you at church and at Sunday school any time you like to come.'

'Thank you very much, Reverend Bell,' they replied. 'And we hope you enjoy the cricket.'

'I can tell that I shall have to tell Mr Grubb and certain others in the village what excellent little cubs you have become.'

The triplets giggled and looked modest.

'Nice to see you, 2.15 and 3.45,' said the vicar. 'Lovely day for a picnic isn't it?'

'Indeed it is,' agreed 2.15, 'and hopefully it will stay fine for the cricket this afternoon.'

'There's a bit of a hitch there, I'm afraid,' explained the Reverend Bell. 'Poor old Bennet, who keeps the village shop, he's hurt his hand and won't be able to play so our team will be one man short.'

'Don't worry,' cried 2.15. 'Sir, there is no problem. I myself will play for the village.'

'Oh how kind,' muttered the vicar.

'Kind indeed,' snapped 3.45. 'Load of nonsense and I'm not staying to watch and look after the children,' and she walked off.

'Oh dear,' said the Reverend Bell, 'I'm afraid I've upset 3.45. But my dear chap, I don't see why you shouldn't play, nothing in the rules about a wolf not playing. Do you know how to play or shall I run through it with you?'

'No need, no need,' cried the wolf. 'I've been watching people playing cricket on that green for hundreds of years. I know how to play better than anyone here. You'll see a display of mastery of the art of cricket as has never been seen before the dreaming spires of your charming church.'

'Well done, 2.15,' beamed the vicar. 'You've saved the day again.'

'Not so fast, not so fast,' interrupted Grandad, 'and who do you think is going to look after the cubs while you're showin' us all the art of cricket?'

'Well, I was hoping one of you people would volunteer.'

'Not me,' said Grandad firmly.

'Oh don't be such an old misery, Bert,' said Gran. 'Don't you worry, 2.15. You leave them right here with Lucy and me. We'll enjoy it, won't we Lucy?'

'Oh yes,' said Lucy in a less than convincing tone.

'Good, then that's settled. All right, my little cublets, you just sit here with Gran and Grandad and do exactly as you're told and watch your clever Daddy play cricket.'

'Well,' said Grandad, 'you two 'ad better entertain our little friends 'ere and I wish you luck.'

Lucy looked hard at the three cubs. 'Do you like skipping?' she asked.

'Oh Auntie Lucy, we don't know what skipping is,' said Romula.

'I'll show you,' said Lucy and picked up her skipping rope.

'Come on, Romula,' she called. 'You try and jump with me.'

So Romula ran into the rope and jumped so well she wore Lucy out.

'Can we have a go?' demanded Remus and Mowgli. 'Please Auntie Lucy, oh please let us.'

'Yes of course,' agreed Lucy. 'Look, I'll hold one end

and Gran the other and then you can all try.'

So soon the three cubs were jumping over the skipping rope and even taking turns holding the ends.

Grandad looked on frowning. 'I don't know if anyone is interested,' he said, 'but 2.15 is about to bat.'

'Our Daddy's going to bat,' cried Mowgli. 'Let's watch him and cheer him on.'

So Lucy and Gran and Grandad sat down under a tree with the three cubs in front of them just in time to see 2.15 dressed in white flannels and shirt, with a cap on his head and guards on his legs, come out of the pavilion carrying a bat.

'Slay them, Daddy,' yelled the cubs, 'slay them.'

'Quiet now,' said Gran. 'Let your Daddy concentrate.'

'We'll be very quiet,' said Remus, and they were.

At the first ball, 2.15 lifted his bat and sent the ball sailing over the boundary.

'Oh, well played,' said Grandad. The triplets cheered.

After a while the cubs were fidgetting about, so Lucy got them skipping again while Grandad kept an eye on the match.

'Well, I don't know,' said Grandad, ' 'e's never played cricket before and 'ee's goin' to score a bloomin' century.'

'How many runs has my Daddy scored?' asked Romula, as she leapt in the air.

'Ninety-six,' Grandad told her. 'Come on and sit down, you lot.'

So they all sat down and watched. The bowler ran up towards 2.15 with the ball and threw it as hard as he could. The ball sailed through the air and while the fielders ran to catch it 2.15 scored four runs.

' 'e's done it, e's scored a century!' yelled Grandad.

The whole crowd stood up and cheered. 2.15 shook hands with the team and acknowledged the acclaim of the crowd.

'Our Daddy's the greatest!' yelled the cubs.

However getting the century seemed to have exhausted 2.15 and after four more runs he was out. The wolf walked back to the pavilion with his bat under his arm, smiling.

'Can we go and see our Daddy?' demanded the cubs.

'All right,' said Gran, 'but only if Romula takes Lucy's hand. Remus come and hold my hand, and Mowgli go with Grandad.'

'Why can't I go on my own?' grumbled Mowgli.

'You just give me your paw and be quiet,' said Grandad roughly. 2.15 treated them all to a lemonade. Soon the whole team were out and it was time for the Muxborough side to go in and bowl.

'All right, my little cublets,' said 2.15. 'Daddy's got to go now and do some fielding. You must go on being very good little cubs. I'm very proud of you.'

2.15 patted them on the head and then ran to start the bowling. He was as good at bowling as he had been at batting. But the cubs were getting bored with the cricket. They began to wander under the tables that had been laid for tea. Gran went off to help the vicar's wife make the teas. Grandad was left in charge. He grabbed Mowgli and Remus by the scruffs of their necks. Romula ran away.

'You can't catch me,' she taunted Grandad.

Just then Lord Muxborough came up. 'Having a bit of trouble, Bert?'

'That Romula has run away,' Grandad told him. 'If you could grab her that might avoid a disaster.

Lord Muxborough set off after Romula but a dog got to Romula first and the two were soon rolling over in the grass, having a great fight.

'Get a bucket of water, someone,' shouted Lord Muxborough.

So while the game went on someone ran up with a bucket of water and threw it over the fighting wolf and the dog. As the water hit her Romula let out a piercing shriek. 2.15 stopped playing and froze in horror. Pete Grubb had chosen that moment to throw the ball at him, but 2.15 was oblivious of everything but his daughter's cry of anguish. The ball sailed through the air.

'Watch out, 2.15!' yelled a few people, but it was too late. The ball travelling at great speed hit 2.15 on the leg. He keeled over and held his leg.

'Ring for an ambulance!' ordered Grandad, as everyone rushed onto the pitch. Someone folded a jacket and put it under 2.15's head and a concerned crowd gathered round him.

'3.45,' said 2.15, 'someone must go and tell her she must come and fetch the children.'

'Don't worry, 2.15,' said Lucy, trying not to cry, 'I'll go.'

'My babies,' whispered the wolf, 'are they all right?'

Grandad put Mowgli and Remus down and Lord Muxborough held out the dripping Romula.

'I had a fight with a dog,' Romula announced to her father proudly. 'The only way they could think of to save the dog's life was to throw water all over us. Aren't I a brave little wolf?'

'Why did you shriek like that, my little elfling?' asked 2.15 faintly.

' 'Cos the water was very cold,' Romula told him indignantly.

'And why were you fighting with the dog?' asked her father.

'The dog started it,' she assured him. 'It was just self-defence.'

'It was, it was,' Remus and Mowgli assured him. 'Poor little Romula was attacked.

Just then the ambulance drove up and a stretcher was rushed over to 2.15. Very gently they lifted 2.15 onto it.

'Where's my Daddy going?' asked Remus.

'He's being taken to hospital, so that they can mend his leg,' Gran explained.

'No, no,' yelled Romula, 'you mustn't allow my Daddy to be taken away.'

The three cubs clung to the stretcher.

'Put me down a minute,' instructed 2.15.

'Now, my little ones,' he said gently. 'Daddy has to go to hospital. But you will come and see me there. Now go quietly with Gran and Grandad, and Mummy will come and fetch you soon. Now make Daddy extra proud of you by being very brave.'

So the cubs clung miserably to Gran and Grandad, waving goodbye to 2.15 as he was put in the ambulance and it sped away into the distance.

6

The Invalid

Shortly after the ambulance had left, Lucy returned to the cricket pitch with 3.45.

'Oh Mummy, Mummy, Daddy's hurt his leg,' cried Romula.

'And he said to be brave and not cry and we were,' said Mowgli, tears running down his face.

3.45 gave them all a hug and a kiss and told them that everything was going to be all right.

'I suppose I'd better go to that hospital full of people to be with 2.15,' she sighed.

'I'll run you there in the car,' volunteered Grandad.

'Can we come, oh please let us come,' begged the triplets.

'Oh, I don't think that would be a good idea,' said Gran hurriedly. 'They're not very keen on children in hospitals, not even human children.'

'We'll keep the children with us till Grandad gets back,' said Gran. 'Don't you worry about that, 3.45, they're quite used to us now, aren't you children?'

'I want to go with my Mummy,' complained Remus.

'I want to see my Daddy,' continued Romula.

'I want to go with my Mummy *and* see my Daddy,' yelled Mowgli.

'Well you can't,' said 3.45 firmly. 'And that's that. Now be good cubs and I'll pick you up as soon as I can.'

Grandad got into the car. 3.45 sat in the front seat next to him.

'Now will you explain to me just what happened?' asked 3.45.

'Well it was like this,' started Grandad. '2.15 did very well and 'e scored a century, a hundred runs, very good that is. Then it was 'is turn to bowl.'

'Why did he have to do that if he'd already done so well?' demanded 3.45.

'I expect 'e wanted the village to win the cricket match, 3.45, you can't blame him for that.'

'I can,' said 3.45. 'Always interfering in everyone's business. I can't find a way of curing him of this happy-ever-after nonsense.'

'Once out of a fairy tale, always out of a fairy tale, I suppose,' said Grandad, as they drove into the hospital car park. They got out of the car and walked into the entrance hall. The man at the reception desk shouted at Grandad:

'Hey, where are you going? No dogs allowed in this hospital.'

'She isn't a dog,' explained Grandad. 'This is 3.45, she's a wolf and her husband 2.15 has just been brought into this hospital because he broke his leg playing cricket.'

'Are you nuts or something?' shouted the man. 'Now get out of here before I call the police, and don't you come in here drunk again.'

'You be quiet, you horrid little man,' snarled 3.45. 'Now tell me where my husband is or I'll bite your ears off. Look on your list and tell me·where I can find 2.15.'

The terrified man looked at his list. 'He's in the men's orthopaedic on the fifth floor,' said a very shaky voice as he hid under the desk.

Eventually they found 2.15 lying in bed with his leg in plaster and held up by a pulley.

'My love, my love,' he called out, 'you have come at last.'

'Huh,' snapped 3.45, 'and you're lucky that I have. You look a right mess, lying here in a ward full of people with your leg up in that whatsit.'

'I'm sorry, my love. I just wasn't looking when the ball was thrown to me – you see I heard Romula scream and I looked up.'

'I've heard all about that,' said 3.45. 'And why were you playing cricket instead of looking after your children? Don't give me that guff about being a man short. If you hadn't been off enjoying yourself, Romula would never have got into that fight with the dog. You needn't expect any sympathy from me.'

'No, my love, but it would be nice if you could spare a little kiss.'

'You're soft, that's what you are,' complained 3.45 as

she kissed him. 'Now you lie down and get a little sleep and I'll come tomorrow and bring the children. They all send their love and are looking forward to seeing you.'

'The hours between now and then will feel long and bleak,' said 2.15. 'Farewell my love, parting is such sweet sorrow. And my love, on the way out would you mind telling them that I am a vegetarian.'

As 3.45 marched out with Grandad the patients huddled under their bedclothes.

'Oh dear,' muttered Grandad, 'something tells me there's going to be some problems keeping a wolf in 'ospital.'

When they got home Mowgli and Remus were happily sliding down the banisters. Romula was nowhere to be seen.

'Where is she?' demanded 3.45.

'I hope you don't mind, 3.45, but Romula insisted on going round to see Pete Grubb, because he was feeling so bad about hitting poor 2.15. She's still there.'

'Grrr,' growled 3.45, 'I'll go and fetch her and if he's hurt a hair of her head I'll eat him in one gulp.'

'I'll go,' said Grandad hurriedly. 'You sit down and have a nice cup of tea, 3.45. I'll go.'

'Yes,' added Gran quickly, 'you've had a trying time. Let Bert go.'

Grandad rushed off followed by Lucy. 'I do hope Romula is all right,' Lucy told her grandfather.

'Not 'arf,' agreed Grandad, 'I mean 'e doesn't like wolves and 'e doesn't like children and Romula's both.'

When they got to the Grubb household a scene of complete harmony met their eyes. Lily Grubb was knitting and Romula was sitting on Pete Grubb's knee.

'Evenin' Pete, evenin' Lily,' said Grandad.

'How's 2.15?' asked Pete Grubb anxiously.

'Yes, how is my poor Daddy?' asked Romula.

'As well as can be expected,' Grandad told them. 'He's in bed with 'is leg all strapped up but he doesn't seem to be in any pain. Come on Romula, your Mum's waiting for you.'

'But I want to stay with my Uncle Pete and my Auntie Lily,' protested Romula.

'Oh, she's such a little love,' crooned Pete Grubb.

'Have another little cakey, poppet,' said Lily Grubb.

'She's got to come,' Grandad insisted. '3.45 is a bit anxious and we shouldn't keep her waiting.'

'Fair enough,' said Pete Grubb. 'Off you go, darling, off you go to your Mummy and come and visit us any time you want. There's always a welcome for you here.'

'Oh thank you, Uncle Pete. Can I give you a big kissy?'

So she kissed Pete and Lily Grubb and went off with Lucy and Grandad singing the praises of Pete Grubb.

'I never was more surprised in my life, Mavis, and that's a fact,' said Grandad after the wolves had gone home. 'Pete Grubb and a baby wolf all coochie, coochie. It's very confusin'. I'm tellin' you, Mavis, wonders will never cease.'

The next day Grandad took 3.45 and the triplets to the hospital. The triplets jumped up at their father.

'Oh Daddy, look at your leg.'

'Daddy, Daddy, give me a kiss.'

'Oh Daddy, look at that funny pulley, can I swing on it?'

'Get down and sit still the lot of you,' snapped 3.45. So the cubs sat silently at the foot of 2.15's bed.

'Well?' demanded 3.45. 'What does the doctor have to say? How long are you going to be stuck in this people's ward?'

'The situation, my dear, is rather complicated. You see,

70

they don't know how long it takes for a wolf's legs to mend and I could not shed any light on the matter. They don't seem to think it will take less than a couple of weeks.'

'Nothing complicated about that,' sniffed 3.45.

'No, my love, but I fear that there may be some problems about my remaining in this ward. The presence of a wolf seems to make the inhabitants of this place of sickness just a touch uneasy.'

'Yes,' chipped in Grandad, 'and four more comin' to visit them probably doesn't make them feel any better about it.'

'But Grandpa Bert, there's no one in any of the beds,' cried Remus.

'I can't see one single person,' squeaked Romula.

'They must all have got better in a hurry,' concluded Mowgli.

'Seems unlikely,' growled 3.45 and she began to prowl around.

Mowgli jumped up on a bed and peered under a sheet. 'There's someone here,' he called.

Remus jumped up on another bed. 'I think there's someone here too. They giggled when I tickled.'

'Let me have a go,' cried Romula. And she jumped up and down in the middle of a bed.

'Get off my tummy,' came a voice.

'This ward is full of people and they're all hiding,' sniffed 3.45.

At that moment a deputation of doctors and nurses marched into the ward and stopped at 2.15's bed. One of the doctors stepped forward. She cleared her throat.

'Mr 2.15, I'm afraid I shall have to ask you to leave this hospital. I'm sorry about this but the staff and patients aren't used to wolves and they all feel very anxious. I

71

would like to emphasize that you have done nothing wrong. On the contrary you have been a perfect patient.'

'You're going to keep him here till he's better or I'll eat you,' snapped 3.45, baring her teeth. 'Get it?'

'No, my love, no,' interrupted 2.15. 'This poor lady is only doing her duty. Now I myself feel uneasy in this place. I'm sure I can manage to limp out if you would be so kind as to unhook my leg.'

'You sit still, 2.15,' said Grandad. 'Now look 'ere, doctor, this wolf is a very well behaved wolf. He's a fairy tale wolf and you were readin' about him when you were about as old as those cubs there. Now 'e needs to be looked after by someone who knows about fractures. Now if 'e can't stay in this 'ospital, what about the local vet?'

'A splendid idea,' said 2.15.

'I'll go and ask 'im,' said Grandad. 'I'll be back as fast as I can.'

Twenty minutes later Grandad returned with a jolly looking woman.

'I say,' she said in a hearty voice, 'you must be 2.15. I was frightfully sorry to hear about your accident.'

'Thank you,' said 2.15 as he shook her hand.

'Yes,' she continued, pumping his paw, 'and I'm so thrilled you want to come over to me instead of staying here.'

'Only if it doesn't inconvenience you,' said 2.15.

'It better hadn't,' snapped 3.45.

'I should absolutely love it,' said the vet. 'My name is Margaret Higgins and I've been dying to meet you, so this accident is a positive bonus for me. Every cloud has a silver lining. Now listen, I've got my animal ambulance downstairs, no problem getting you over to my place.'

Turning to the doctors she asked, 'Could you lend me a

72

trolley to get 2.15 downstairs and into my van?'

'Well, I'm not sure about that,' said the doctor hesitatingly.

3.45 growled menacingly.

'Sir,' cried 2.15, 'I would be for ever in your debt if you would loan me one of your trolleys for a mere five minutes.'

'Oh very well,' said the doctor, 'on condition that you never come back here again.'

'Sir,' replied 2.15 with dignity, as the vet and Grandad lifted him onto a trolley, 'nothing, nothing in the whole world would ever persuade me to return here, have no fear.'

So 2.15 left the ward on a trolley pushed by the vet and with his leg supported by Grandad and 3.45 and the cubs following the little procession.

'Good riddance,' someone yelled.

'Yeh, and never come back,' called another.

2.15 bit his lip. 'Gentlemen,' he said, as he reached the door, 'I wish you all a speedy recovery. Good day.'

Soon they were all installed in the vet's friendly kitchen. 2.15 was ensconced on a couch with lots of pillows supporting his leg. Margaret Higgins made tea and crumpets dripping with butter for everyone. The cubs ate lots and lots and then curled up in front of the fire and went to sleep. 3.45 sat by 2.15 and held his hand: 'You'll get well here,' she said. 'I know you will.'

'Don't worry about a thing, 3.45,' said the vet, 'I'll take the best care of him anyone could. You can't imagine what a thrill it is for me to be able to talk to an animal after all the years I've been involved with them. 2.15, you'll have to tell me when you're tired or I'll keep you up all night nattering.'

'Thanks,' said 3.45 gruffly.

'And you're welcome here any time, 3.45. If I'm out on visits or in the surgery, just let yourself in and eat whatever you find in the fridge, and the cubs can come any time they want too. I don't mind keeping an eye on them if you've got other things to do.'

'It's very disturbing,' grumbled 3.45.

'What's disturbing, my love?' asked 2.15.

'Nice people,' muttered 3.45. 'They confuse me. It shouldn't be allowed. First there was Lucy, then Gran and Grandad, and the Muxboroughs are all right, and now there's you.'

'Sorry, I'll see what I can do about being horrid,' chortled Margaret Higgins.

Under the vet's tender care 2.15 began to get better quickly. In the evening over cocoa he would tell her all about his life as a wolf and his life as a dog.

'Oh really,' exclaimed the vet, 'how interesting. I'll write a book about it. Then maybe people will treat animals better.'

3.45 who was visiting sniffed contemptuously.

'3.45 doesn't think much of people,' 2.15 explained. 'She was in the zoo for a long time, you see.'

'Oh really, how absolutely fascinating.'

'Fascinating!' snapped 3.45. 'There was nothing fascinating about it. It was very boring and I don't like to think about it.'

'Sorry 3.45,' said Margaret Higgins, 'I didn't mean to tread on your eh, toes.'

'Waste of time, people, a complete waste of time,' declared 3.45, and she strode off.

'Oh dear,' said the vet, 'I didn't mean to hurt her feelings and spark off bad memories.'

'She's always afraid someone will take her back to the zoo,' explained 2.15. 'I rescued her you see. We fell in love and had to live happily ever after.'

'And you have,' smiled the vet.

'Give or take a cricket ball or two,' smiled 2.15.

'I wish she would tell me about her experiences in the zoo,' mused the vet. 'It might make some impact on people.'

'You mean get zoos abolished.'

'Well no, I think that might be a bit much to hope for, but the animals might get treated better.'

'I'll have a word with her,' promised 2.15. 'You have to pick just the right moment with 3.45.'

The vet was a bit surprised a few days later when 3.45 strode in. 'I've come to dictate my memoirs,' 3.45 informed the vet. 'I haven't got all day, so get out your tape recorder or note book or whatever people use for such things and let's get on with it.'

'Oh 3.45,' exclaimed Margaret Higgins, 'this is absolutely wonderful of you. I mean I don't know what to say. After all you've been through.'

'Shut up,' snapped 3.45, 'or I'll go; no time to listen to people wittering on.'

So the vet got out her tape recorder and 3.45 talked for nearly three hours. Margaret Higgins listened enwrapped.

'So I got rescued and that's the end. You got what you wanted and now I'll be off.'

The vet had tears in her eyes: 'Thank you so much, 3.45,' she said taking the wolf's paw for a moment. 'That was very moving. It was jolly brave of you to do it. I'll see to it that it gets published.'

'Better had,' grumbled 3.45. 'Haven't got time to waste, you know,' and she ran off back into the forest.

2.15 was getting better so fast that he returned to his family in the forest, although he was still limping quite severely. Every evening he came to see the vet and she gave him exercises and massage and heat treatment.

'My leg's nearly better,' 2.15 informed Margaret Higgins. 'You are a splendid vet. I shall recommend you highly to the beasts of the forest. You have the 2.15 seal of approval.'

'Thanks,' said the vet blushing. 'Jolly nice of you to say so. By the way, 2.15, here's the piece I wrote from 3.45's testament. Perhaps you could give it to her.'

'I can't wait to read it,' said 2.15. '3.45 would never talk to me about her experiences. I was amazed that she was willing to talk to you.'

The next day when 2.15 came for his treatment, 3.45 was with him, clutching a bunch of wild flowers. She thrust them into the vet's hands.

'For you,' she said briskly. 'All that talking – it made me feel better.'

'Thanks,' said the vet.

'And now, after all that you've done for us,' said 2.15, '3.45 and I think we should do something for you. We think you should live happily ever after and we're going to work on it.'

'But I'm very happy as I am,' the vet explained. 'I love my work, I love my house, I've got lots of friends and enough money. I'm fine.'

'That's all well and good,' smiled 2.15, 'but it's not the same as living happily ever after.'

'I think she ought to have some cubs,' commented 3.45.

'But I don't want to have any cubs, I mean children,' complained the vet. 'I just want to get on with my life.'

'That's what you say,' cried 2.15, 'but nonetheless 3.45 and I shall feel honour bound to repay your great kindness to us in true fairy tale fashion. I'm afraid nothing but living happily ever after will do. So prepare yourself.'

And leaving the vet with her mouth hanging open, the two wolves pranced off into the forest.

7

Vive La France

'Look,' Grandad said to Lucy one morning, 'a card from François Perrier. He's inviting us all to visit him in France.'

'François who?'

'You know,' said Grandad, 'Gaston Loup, the French onion seller. Only 'is real name is François Perrier.'

'Oh,' said Lucy, studying the card, 'and he wants 2.15 and family to go as well.'

'I'd love to go,' sighed Grandad. 'I 'aven't been to France since I landed there on D-Day. And I bet Mavis would love to go and all.'

'Let's go then,' said Lucy. 'A day trip doesn't cost very much. He says he lives just near Calais and he'd meet us in his car and guide us to his place.'

'Why not?' agreed Grandad. 'If your Mum and Dad agree, let's do that. Give ourselves a treat.'

Gran was enthusiastic and Lucy got permission to go.

'I'd better go and look for 2.15 and see if he wants to join us,' added Lucy.

'Do you think it's a good idea?' questioned Grandad. 'I mean 'e'd never know if we went without him. If 2.15 comes there'll be trouble and don't deny it.'

'Come on, Bert,' protested Gran, '2.15 has been invited so it should be his decision.'

'Oh, all right,' groaned Grandad.

'I'll go and look for him,' said Lucy, and she went

through the forest calling out for the wolf. After a while 2.15 jumped out.

'We've had a card from France, from François Perrier, you know, Gaston Loup. He's invited us all to France to visit him, and he wants you to come too with the family.'

'That's a good idea,' cried the wolf. 'I would love to roam in foreign lands and sample some of the more unusual French cuisine. Tell him we would be honoured to accept.'

So a week later Gran, Grandad and Lucy were sitting in the car with the five wolves in the back. When they got to the boat, they left the car below deck and went upstairs. 3.45 had been very suspicious of the trip, claiming that French or English people were people and that they were all a waste of time and ought to be eaten. She decided to stay in the car with the sleeping cubs. 2.15 stood on deck and looked out to sea. His eyes had a far-away look and he didn't talk much.

'Something up, 2.15?' asked Grandad. 'You worried about not being able to speak French?'

'No, nothing like that,' replied the wolf.

'If you think you're going to be sea-sick I could let you have some pills,' Gran told him.

'No, it's not that either. I'm worried because of what is happening to my forest.'

'What are you on about?' demanded Grandad. 'What is 'appening to your forest?'

'That's just it,' explained 2.15. 'I don't understand it but it is disturbing. Lots of the trees are dying and it seems to be getting worse all the time.'

'Yeh!' said Grandad, 'Now that you mention it, I've noticed too.'

'It's acid rain,' Lucy told them. 'I saw a programme

about it and then my teacher made us do a project on it.'

'Come on then,' said 2.15, 'tell us about it. At last your television watching and all this going to school nonsense has been of some use.'

'Well,' began Lucy, 'all the factories and power stations and the cars put out all sorts of chemicals and gases into the air. Then when it rains the chemicals mix with the raindrops and they drop on the leaves of the trees and the trees don't like the chemicals and they die.'

'Ah,' cried 2.15, 'so if the factories and the power stations and the cars stopped putting all these chemicals into the atmosphere then the trees would be all right again?'

'I suppose so,' said Lucy.

'Then the problem is solved,' declared the wolf. 'I shall go and explain to everyone that my forest is in danger and then they will control the chemicals. I would appreciate it if none of you mentioned this to 3.45. I don't want to worry her.'

So they all promised, and soon they saw France peeping over the horizon.

'It looks just like England from the sea,' said 2.15 in a disappointed tone.

'That's true,' agreed Lucy, 'but it won't seem so once we land.'

They drove off the boat and there, shouting and waving, was François Gaston Perrier Loup.

'Ah 2.15, mon vieil ami,' cried the onion seller. 'How wonderful to see you! Welcome, bienvenu en France.'

'Merci, cher ami,' cried 2.15. 'Let me introduce you to my wife, 3.45, and my three little ones, Romula, Remus and Mowgli.'

'Bonjour monsieur,' chorused the triplets.

'Ah, zey speak French, ze leetle ones,' cried the Frenchman.

'Well no,' replied 2.15, 'not exactly. But I taught them a few words for the occasion.'

'Ah!' said François. 'And this is your charming wife. Enchanté, madame,' and he kissed 3.45's paw.

'Huh,' muttered 3.45, trying not to look pleased. 'Maybe French people and English people are not quite the same after all.'

The party set off for François' house. His wife Arlette had prepared a meal for them with lots of snails and frogs' legs. 2.15 was delighted: 'Dear friends, what wonderful people you are. Today I shall dine as I have dreamed of doing and still be a vegetarian.'

'I'm not eatin' that,' sniffed Grandad. 'And that's final.'

'No problem, my friend,' cried their host. 'For you Arlette has prepared something a leetle more convention-al.'

So they sat round outside and ate. It was autumn but it was still warm and they all ate and drank to their hearts' content. 2.15 proposed a toast:

'Vive la France.'

Everyone joined in. Then Grandad began to nod off.

'I think I'll have a little sleep too,' said Gran.

'Bien sur, of course,' said Arlette.

The cubs were playing with the tablecloth. Lucy could see that a disaster was imminent.

'3.45,' she said quickly, 'I'd love to go for a walk in the woods. Would you like to come with the cubs?'

'A splendid idea,' cried 2.15. 'Don't you think so, my love?'

'Anything's better than being with people,' growled 3.45. 'Come on, children, we're going for a walk.'

So the wolves and Lucy went walking in the woods behind the house. The cubs wanted to play hide-and-seek, so they hid and the other three looked for them. After a while 3.45 gathered the cubs together and they turned back to the house. 2.15 walked alongside them looking distracted and not saying anything.

'You all right, 2.15?' asked Lucy.

'Humm,' said 2.15 absent-mindedly. 'Oh, eh, fine thanks.'

'You don't seem it. What's wrong?'

'It's these trees,' explained 2.15. 'They're just like the trees in our forest, and acid rain must fall here too.'

'Yes,' agreed Lucy, 'it does look like it and I heard at school that it is happening all over Europe.'

'This is very worrying,' said 2.15 shaking his head. 'I shall have to do some homework and then decide on a course of action.'

'I don't see what you can do about it,' said Lucy. 'I mean it's a very big problem. It would take more than one wolf to solve it.'

'We shall see about that,' replied 2.15. 'We shall see.'

When they returned to the house, Gran and Grandad were about to have tea.

'Come and sit down,' cried their host. 'We 'ave just made ze English tea. Come and join us.'

'Come and drink up,' said Gran. 'We'll have to go soon and catch the boat back.'

Shortly afterwards they were speeding towards Calais. As they reached the boat, a sailor ran towards them.

'Stop there, stop, you can't take dogs to England. There's rules about rabies.'

'Rabies?' whispered 2.15. 'What's rabies?'

'Sometimes dogs get rabid,' Grandad explained, 'and then if they bite someone the person dies.'

'Your dogs will have to go into quarantine for six months,' said the sailor.

'I'm not going into quarantine,' whispered 2.15. 'Think of something to do quickly.'

'We've changed our minds,' Gran decided. 'We'll catch the night ferry.

Gran, Grandad, Lucy and the five wolves all drove off to find the British Consul. As they all lined up in front of his desk, the Consul smiled at them.

'Good evening,' he said to Gran and Grandad. 'What can I do for you?'

'It is I who need your help,' said 2.15 stepping forward. 'My wife and myself and our three little ones have just spent the day with a dear friend in France. We now wish to return to our home in Britain, but do not wish to spend six months in quarantine.'

'Well quite,' said the Consul. 'It would be most tedious and inconvenient.'

'I'm so glad you understand,' said 2.15.

'No problem about that,' said the Consul. 'What I don't understand is how you can talk.'

'Sir,' declared 2.15, 'I am the wolf from the story Little Red Riding Hood, so of course I speak most excellent English.'

'A character from a fairy story, eh?' said the Consul grinning. 'You meet all sorts in this job but you are the first, the very first character from a story. It is a pleasure, a very great pleasure to meet you.'

'Thank you, sir, but can you help us? If we cannot get into Britain as animals, can you provide us with passports so that we can return to our home as people?'

'Not me,' growled 3.45. 'I'd rather stay in France than pretend to be a person.'

'I'm very sorry,' said the Consul, 'but I don't think I can

give you passports. In the first place you aren't human beings and secondly I am not at all sure that you are British citizens.'

'I must be British,' said 2.15, 'after all I live in a British forest. And 3.45 and the babes were all born in Britain, and what is more, I'm an old friend of the Queen's.'

'Come to think of it, you're an old friend of mine,' said the Consul. 'Look, I'd like to help but I just don't see how I can. The way I look at it is that you're a citizen of the world, not of one particular country.'

'Umm,' said 2.15, 'I like that thought. Now tell me how does a citizen of the world get a passport for himself and his family?'

'Oh,' said the Consul, 'it's not a legal status, it's just an honorary title, no help in getting around from A to B.'

'Well,' said 2.15, 'I can see that we shall just have to stay here in France after all. Thank you, sir, for your time and advice.'

They filed out of the Consulate and went to a café. Gran, Grandad and Lucy sat round the table and the wolves lay at their feet.

'Are you really going to stay in France?' Lucy whispered to 2.15.

'No, of course not,' he whispered back. 'You should all go home before your ticket expires. Go to that big hotel in Dover, that very big white one, and wait in the lounge. I'll phone you there.'

So Gran, Grandad and Lucy got on the night boat and waved goodbye to the wolves. Tears ran down Lucy's face.

'Wouldn't it be terrible if we never met them again?' she said.

'Don't you take on, Lucy,' Grandad reassured her. 'We've not seen the end of them, not by a long chalk.'

They went to the hotel in Dover and waited in the lounge. Eventually the clerk at the desk called out:

'Call for a Miss Lucy Jones.'

Lucy leapt up:

'That's me,' she cried and grabbed the phone.

'Is that Red Riding Hood?' came a familiar voice from the other end of the phone. 'This is your destiny speaking. Meet me on the small beach under the castle at midnight. See you then.'

So by midnight Gran, Grandad and Lucy huddled together on the beach, a lantern lit, and wrapped in a blanket. Gran kept handing out hot coffee from the thermos.

'It's midnight,' said Grandad, 'and I can't 'ear a bloomin' thing.'

'I think I can hear oars,' said Gran.

'Look,' said Lucy, 'right out there. I'm sure I saw a boat.'

For a while there was silence. Then Lucy noticed lights moving down the path to the cove.

'It must be the police,' said Gran. 'Oh dear, they have chosen the wrong time to come. There's no way to signal to 2.15. We'll say we're just having a picnic and hope that 2.15 and family don't turn up in the middle.'

'Don't see 'ow they could turn up,' said Grandad, 'not unless they're swimmin' from France.'

'What's going on down here, then?' came a loud voice.

'We're just having a picnic, officer,' said Gran.

'Bit chilly isn't it?' asked the policeman.

'We're keeping warm with some coffee,' said Gran. 'Would you like a cup?'

'Sounds good,' replied the policeman.

Suddenly Lucy heard a loud splashing sound coming from the sea. She thought quickly. 'Do you like that song

about the policeman?' she asked brightly.'You know the one that goes: "A policeman's lot is not a happy one".'

'Happy one,' echoed Gran and Grandad.

The policeman looked at them in amazement.

'Do you agree with that?' Lucy asked.

'With what?' asked the policeman.

'That a policeman's lot is not a happy one,' sang Lucy, Gran and Grandad together at the tops of their voices.

'Well no,' said the policeman and quickly finished his coffee. 'I'll be getting along now. I suggest you do the same. It's a bit suspicious sitting on a beach all night.'

'Don't you worry officer, we'll be going home in a minute,' said Gran.

'Oh well done,' said a voice from the darkness. 'That was quick thinking.'

'2.15, is that you?' asked Gran, as Grandad turned the lantern in the direction of the voice.

'Of course it's me,' came the muffled voice.

Suddenly in front of them stood a frogman. He lifted off the plastic facepiece and there was the wolf's face.

'Help me out,' he gasped, 'I can't move in this thing.'

So they helped him out of the frogman suit, and folded it up and gave it to Lucy to carry. Then they walked up the path back to the castle and 2.15 bounded along barking in his best dog's voice. At the top the policeman was waiting.

'Glad you decided to come up. I wasn't happy about you lot down there on your own.'

'We were just waiting for our dog to come back,' explained Grandad.

'Nice dog,' said the policeman, patting 2.15 on the head. The wolf licked him enthusiastically. 'Friendly too, isn't he?'

'Too flippin' friendly,' said Grandad. 'Come on Lucy,

we've got to find the car and get orf 'ome.'

Once in the car they showered 2.15 with questions: 'Where's 3.45?' 'Are they coming back a different way?' 'How did you get the frogman suit?'

'It's all very simple,' said the wolf. 'I borrowed the frogman suit. A friend of François lent it to me and a fisherman friend dropped me off here. Now let's hurry back home and arrange for the return of my dear wife and children.'

'2.15, how are you going to do that?'

'I have just worked out a plan,' replied 2.15, 'with my usual flair and genius. Just put your foot on the pedal. We must be back by 3.00 in the morning.'

'Why?' said Lucy.

'You will see, dear child.'

They were back by 2.30. 2.15 insisted that they drive to the field near Muxborough Hall.

'Come on,' said the wolf, 'help me light a fire.'

Grandad grumbled as he collected wood in the car headlights: 'I don't know what you're plannin', 2.15. But something tells me it's a bad idea.'

'On the contrary, dear friend,' said the wolf, lighting the bonfire, 'it is a brilliant idea.'

For a while nothing happened, then suddenly there was the sound of a plane overhead. Lucy looked up and noticed that a parachute was hanging over the field and slowly floating down. Then she noticed three more tiny parachutes.

'So that's it. You're parachuting them back.'

'Exactly so,' said 2.15.

A moment later 3.45 landed and then Remus, Mowgli and lastly Romula.

'That was lovely,' squeaked Romula, as she fought her way out of the parachute. 'Can I do it again?'

'Don't be silly,' said 3.45. 'Now that we're home at last, we're going to stay on dry land.'

'But it was such fun, Mummy,' chorused the cubs.

'Yes, darlings,' said 2.15. 'But now we're back in our own dear forest. Come on, let's go and get some sleep. Goodnight, Gran and Grandad and Lucy, thanks so much for all your help.'

'Night,' said Grandad, as he watched them disappear. 'I think a bit of sleep is a good idea. Come on let's go 'ome too.'

8

The T.V. Star

The demand for visits to Muxborough Hall was so great that Lord Muxborough decided to open it for the weeks leading up to Christmas. Gran and Grandad made loads of apple dishes to sell. 2.15 talked to people and had his photograph taken endlessly.

'I'm a bit bored with it,' he confided to Lucy, 'but I promised I'd put Muxborough Hall on the map and I must see it through.'

'But the tourists really love you, 2.15,' Lucy reminded him. 'They all see you as an old friend from their childhood.'

'I know,' said 2.15. 'It's quite amazing, wherever they come from it's the same, Germany, France, America. It gives me a special place in their lives. You know Lucy, I could have quite an important influence on people for the good.'

'Sorry, I don't follow.'

'Oh dear. You always were a bit slow,' sighed the wolf. 'About the acid rain and my forest dying and other forests dying, if I explained to the people in power, maybe they'd put a stop to it. They might listen to me rather than anyone else because I'm an old friend. Now I must be the only old friend whom they all have in common. If I put my mind to it I could do a great deal of good.'

'Umm,' said Lucy dubiously, 'I don't know about that.'

'Of course you don't, dear child,' cried the wolf, 'for you are very young. I shall discuss the matter with Margaret Higgins. She'll help me with my investigations. At the same time I can arrange for her to live happily ever after.'

'But I don't think she wants to live happily ever after, 2.15, not in the way you mean it. Anyway you can't see to it that the whole world lives happily ever after.'

'I can try,' said the wolf. 'I may not succeed but I shall certainly try.'

'What are you planning, 2.15?' asked Lucy. 'I don't understand what you're on about.'

'Don't let that worry you,' said the wolf, 'because you will, you definitely will.'

The next time Lucy saw 2.15 he was sitting with Margaret Higgins with a huge pile of books in front of them.

'Hello, Lucy,' said the vet. '2.15 has got every book on forests, the environment and acid rain out of the library and we're going through them.'

'Yes,' said 2.15, 'and I am making copious notes because it is vital that I have all the facts right if I'm to influence those who make decisions.'

'I still don't know what you're talking about,' complained Lucy.

'Never mind about that. Just put all the books on that chair in a nice neat pile, please Lucy. The librarian is coming to fetch them shortly.'

'Coming to fetch them?' said Margaret Higgins, looking surprised. 'Why should he do that?'

'Well,' said 2.15 mysteriously, 'the librarian is a very pleasant young man and I wanted him to meet you. So I told him my leg was still very painful.'

'Oh 2.15, you are a pain,' cried the vet, 'I've told you I

don't want to get married. It's very embarrassing.'

The door bell rang and there stood the librarian with a box of books.

'Brought all these books for you, 2.15. I'll just grab the others and dash, the girlfriend's waiting in the car. Bye.'

'Bye,' said 2.15, looking very downcast.

'See,' said Margaret Higgins cheerfully, 'now no more of this nonsense.'

'Madam,' said the wolf bowing down low, 'reluctantly I accede to your request.'

Just then came a loud noise from outside, the back door was flung open and a strange man staggered in with his hands above his head. Behind him came 3.45 snarling fiercely.

'My love, my love!' cried 2.15, running over to her. 'Has he treated you badly? The brute. Shall I bite him for you?'

'I haven't done anything,' said the man in a terrified tone.

'Is that true dearest?' asked 2.15.

'Yes,' growled 3.45, 'I brought him here for her.'

'Oh how sweet,' smiled 2.15. 'You see, even 3.45 wants you to live happily ever after.'

'Don't,' snapped 3.45. 'Just think she should have some cubs.'

The man sat down on the nearest chair.

'Would someone or some wolf tell me what this is all about?'

'I'm terribly sorry you've been bothered,' said Margaret Higgins. 'It's quite unforgivable but 2.15 and 3.45 want to marry me off.'

'Oh,' said the man, 'do you need their help?'

'No,' said the vet indignantly.

'Sir,' said 2.15 grandly, 'may I offer my apologies to you

92

on behalf of myself and my dear wife. We were trying to do good.'

'All right then,' grumbled the man. 'As you're out of a fairy tale I'll overlook it. Now may I go home?'

'Of course,' said the vet, 'and I'm terribly sorry about all this nonsense.'

2.15 and the vet stood on the doorstep and waved him goodbye.

'Go to all that trouble for you and you just show him out,' grumbled 3.45. 'Grrrr!'

'Both of you have got to stop this,' said the vet, 'or I shall get very angry.'

'Shan't,' muttered 3.45.

The vet looked at the wolf in despair. Just then there was a knock at the door.

'Goodness knows who this is,' said the vet, as she went to open it. There stood another man, with Romula in his arms.

'Excuse me,' he said, 'but I found this puppy in my garden and she has your address on her collar.'

Margaret Higgins took Romula from the man.

'Pretty little thing, isn't she?' he said.

Romula winked at the vet. 'Humm,' she said dubiously. 'Look, I'm very grateful to you for bringing her back. Her parents will be relieved.'

'You're the vet, aren't you?' asked the man.

'Yes, that's right.'

'Let me introduce myself. I'm Andrew Compton and I've been meaning to contact you because I have a sick cat. Could I bring her round?'

'Please do.'

'Would this evening be all right? Then we could have a drink and a chat. I don't know a soul as I've just moved in and I'm pretty lonely.'

'Yes, do call round this evening, that would be lovely,' said Margaret as she waved him goodbye.

'I did it, I did it!' yelled Romula as he drove away. 'Aren't I clever, I'm the one who saw to it that she lives happily ever after.'

'You're jumping to conclusions, Romula,' said Margaret.

'I'm not, I'm not,' squeaked Romula. 'You look all pleased.'

'He did seem rather nice,' conceded the vet.

'Romula,' said 2.15, 'I'm proud of you.'

'Huh,' sniffed 3.45. 'She's going to be just like you, worrying about people all the time. I'm off to find Remus and Mowgli.'

'I'll away with you to the greenwood, fair one,' said 2.15.

'See you tomorrow, Margaret, for I must continue with my research.

2.15 began to borrow more and more books from the library. Every spare moment was spent studying the facts of acid rain and the condition of the forests of the world. Every week he would go round to the vet to borrow her typewriter to record his findings.

'It's all very worrying,' he told her. 'I feel I've got to do something because I want my little ones to have a nice forest to live in and anyway people need forests too.'

'Lots of people agree with you, 2.15. All over the world people are getting together in groups to try and do something about it.'

'I'm glad to hear that,' said the wolf. 'I ought to help them in my unique position as a childhood friend of just about everyone.'

'I have an idea,' said the vet. 'You remember the man who brought Romula to my place a few days ago?'

'Of course,' said 2.15. 'How's that going? I've been so worried about the forest I forgot all about you living happily ever after.'

'Don't worry about that,' said Margaret. 'As it happens we're getting on fine. I only mention it because he works on television and he might be able to help you draw attention to the acid rain.'

'Television!' cried 2.15. 'Perfect, yes. I think the good Andrew Compton may be just the person we seek. Fate has sent him to us.'

'Actually it was Romula,' Margaret reminded him.

'She was merely the instrument of fate. Come, let us go and see the gentleman without further delay.'

'There's a bit of a problem,' the vet told him. 'I didn't tell him about you being a fairy tale character because all that happily ever after stuff was a bit embarrassing.'

'I myself will acquaint him with the facts,' said 2.15. 'All personal considerations must be put behind us.

Come, let us go and recruit him to our cause.'

Shortly they arrived at Andrew Compton's cottage.

'Hello, Margaret,' he said. 'What a nice surprise. Come on in. Ah, I see you've brought one of your patients.'

'No, sir,' declared 2.15. 'I am no longer one of the good lady's patients, she has restored me fully to health. I am a supplicant come to ask for your help and advice in a vital matter.'

'Good grief, the animal can speak. You must be the 2.15 I've been hearing so much about.'

'That is indeed correct. I am he and I need access to the television to make as many people as possible aware of the danger to our forest.'

'You want to go on television? How fantastic, absolutely terrif. You have come to the right man. I've been hearing about you ever since I arrived in this part of the world and I've been meaning to go on your trip round Muxborough Hall and now you've come to me. I'd absolutely love to make a TV programme about you.'

'Good,' said 2.15 grinning, 'because you see I want to talk to people about the dangers from acid rain.'

'Great,' said the television producer. 'Now the sooner we can get you talking about it the better. I think we should begin with the story of your life and how you came to live in the world. Everyone will know you, there can't be anyone in the country who doesn't know the story. You'll be the biggest sensation since sliced bread.'

So in between showing people round Muxborough Hall, 2.15 helped Andrew Compton make the programme. Eventually it was finished and ready to be shown. The evening it was going to be shown, everyone went round to Gran and Grandad's cottage. Lucy and her Mum and Dad, Lord and Lady Muxborough, Pete and Lily Grubb, Margaret Higgins and Andrew Compton, and the five wolves. The first part showed the forest, then 2.15 travelling on the train to London. It traced his footsteps to the flats on the Isle of Dogs, and talked to people who had known him including Sir Samuel Wolf and Mr Al-u-Din. Then came some scenes showing 2.15 taking the tourists around Muxborough Hall.

'It's super,' said Lucy. 'You're very good on TV.'

'Praise indeed,' said 2.15 smiling. 'But now comes the serious bit.'

The next scene showed 2.15 and his family walking and playing in the forest. Then the camera focused in on 2.15 standing under a tree: 'As you have seen I have been living in this beautiful forest for thousands of years. My wife 3.45 and my triplets love it too. But a new and very worrying development is taking place here. Look at this tree, it is dying. All over the forest the same thing is happening. Now I worry that by the time the triplets are grown up wolves there may not be any forest left for them to inhabit and enjoy.'

'Look,' squeaked Romula, 'there's me and my Mummy and the boys.'

'Quiet!' shouted everyone and for once Romula was silenced.

'I know that many people are worried about what is happening and are protesting vigorously but I want to talk tonight to the majority of people who are not doing anything.'

'That's me, I'm afraid,' said Lord Muxborough shame-faced.

'It's all of us, Muffy,' said Gran comfortingly.

'Dear friends,' continued 2.15, 'the forests of Europe are in danger of dying. They are not just places of beauty and joy for people to walk and relax in, they are absolutely essential to the survival of mankind. Trees produce

97

oxygen that we all need to breathe. The death of the forests is not inevitable. It is caused by pollution from cars and power stations. With money and planning and thought the damaging chemicals in the atmosphere could be drastically reduced.'

'I'm going to start a local conservation group, 2.15,' Lucy told the wolf.

'On behalf of wild animals everywhere, I appeal to you, the ordinary people, to do everything you can to protect our habitat. It is in the interests of all of us, men and beasts. Please think about what I have said and act now. Soon it will be too late. Goodnight, and please help me to help you to live happily ever after.'

When it was over the group sat quietly for a minute.

'You were splendid, 2.15,' said Lady Muxborough. 'Absolutely splendid.'

'Well, I spoke from the heart,' 2.15 told her, 'and because I believe that once people really know about the problem things will be done to stop it.'

After the programme the village was flooded with journalists wanting interviews with 2.15 and photographs of him with his family. Letters of support poured in.

'You see,' said 2.15 triumphantly, 'I told you that once people realised what was going on they would rally. The next step in my grand plan is to explain the gravity of the situation to the world's leaders.'

The following week a letter arrived from America. 2.15 looked intently.

'It's from the White House,' he said in an awed tone.

'Fantastic,' said Andrew Compton. 'It's what you've wanted, 2.15. The President of the United States has written to you. Go on, open it.'

Nervously 2.15 ripped open the envelope and read the letter.

'What does it say?' demanded the TV producer.

Dear 2.15,
Seeing you on television the other night took me right back to my childhood. I recalled how my Momma used to tuck me up and tell me the story of Red Riding Hood on winter nights. Just hearing your voice took me right back to those happy days of boyhood. Your plea on behalf of the world's forests went straight to my heart. We would be mighty honoured if you would visit us here in the United States. I would like to invite you to stay right here in the White House with me. Please don't say no, our grandchildren would never get over it. Just let me know when you would like to come and I will arrange for my private presidential jet, Airforce One, to transport you directly to Washington.

'Signed by the President of the United States himself. Cor blimey 2.15,' said Grandad. 'You've gone and done it! The flippin' President wants to talk to you.'

'This is the chance I've been waiting for. I knew I had a special place in the hearts of people.'

As soon as it could be arranged, 2.15 flew off in Airforce One. Grandad and Lucy waved as 2.15 boarded the plane.

'I'll write and phone, dear friends,' he called. 'Take care of 3.45 and the cubs, farewell.'

For days the newspapers and the television were full of 2.15's visit to the U.S.A. There were pictures of 2.15 on the lawn of the White House with the President, in Texas wearing a ten gallon hat, in Arizona at a rodeo, in Hollywood posing with famous stars and on a reservation with American Indians.

' 'e's certainly getting around,' commented Grandad.

'I know,' agreed Lucy, 'but it doesn't seem to have much to do with the world's forests.'

'Well 'e's due 'ome tomorrow,' said Grandad, 'so we'll hear all about it then.'

When they collected 2.15 from the airport he was rather subdued.

'What's up?' asked Grandad. 'It looked like you was 'aving the time of your life.'

'Well,' said 2.15, as they drove home. 'Everyone was very kind but they didn't want to hear much about the forests. I was just a star, a sensation, a nine day wonder on account of being out of a fairy tale. I don't think they took me very seriously. I was just the flavour of the month.'

'You must have made some impact,' said Lucy. 'You worked so hard and went to so many places.'

'Yes,' said the wolf sadly, 'some, but not enough. I shall

have to think of other ways to influence the course of events. Fear not, dear friends, I am not defeated.'

'I think you should stay in the forest for a while with 3.45 and the cubs,' said Lucy. 'It's not fair on them if you're always away.'

'You're right, of course,' agreed the wolf. 'I shall return to my loved ones and my duties as a father for a while. But I shall not let the matter rest, it is too important. The world will hear once more from 2.15, spokes-animal of the other creatures who share this planet with people.'

9

The Note

Early one morning Lucy was woken by a loud tapping. Half asleep she got up and opened the window. 3.45 stood outside waving a piece of paper impatiently.

'Hello, 3.45,' she said sleepily. 'What do you want?'

'Read that,' said 3.45, thrusting the piece of paper into Lucy's hands. 'I haven't learned to read yet. You don't need to in the zoo.'

'Come in,' said Lucy taking the paper from the wolf. As 3.45 climbed in the window Lucy studied the paper.

'It's in 2.15's writing,' she observed.

'I know that,' snapped 3.45. 'But what does it say?'

Lucy drew the curtains back and read out:

My dearest love,

By the time you get this note I will have gone off on a great mission to save the world. I have to do this in order to see that our forest will be safe for our little ones. I may be gone for a while but don't worry, I am a citizen of the world and I am sure I will be welcomed and cared for wherever I go. I am sorry to leave you to look after the cubs but it is for their sake that I am doing this. Knowing you to be the best mother in the world, I feel quite easy about leaving them. Tell Lord Muxborough I'll be back at work as soon as I can.

Love and kisses, 2.15.

'I'll chew him to pieces when he comes back,' growled 3.45. 'Do you have any idea where he's gone?'

'None,' answered Lucy. 'I wish I did. I'll get dressed and clean my teeth and we'll go and see if Gran or Grandad knows anything.'

Lucy left a note for her Mum and Dad and set off with 3.45.

'You go on,' said 3.45. 'I'll go and get the cubs and meet you at Gran's house.'

Gran and Grandad were having breakfast when Lucy arrived.

'2.15's disappeared,' Lucy told them. 'He left this note for 3.45.'

'Oh dear, oh lor,' said Grandad. 'Where's 'e gone? 'as anyone any ideas?'

'One thing's sure,' said Gran. 'It's got something to do with his concern about the forests and the acid rain.'

'3.45 and the cubs are coming round,' Lucy told her, 'then we can pool our ideas and hold a council of war.'

'I'll put the kettle on,' said Grandad, 'and make a pile of toast.'

When 3.45 arrived they all sat round talking:

'Do you think he's gone to see the Queen?' asked Gran.

'Not likely,' said Lucy. 'That wouldn't take so long.'

'Mummy, Mummy, can I go and see my Uncle Pete?' asked Romula.

'Huh,' sniffed 3.45, 'all right, you can go but don't bother him. I'm very short tempered today and I might eat someone.'

'Yes, Mummy,' said Romula and bounced off.

'2.15 could have gone anywhere,' said Gran, 'back to France, to Spain or Germany or Italy, anywhere.'

'Yeh,' said Grandad gloomily, 'or South America, or

Australia or the North Pole.'

'I just don't know where to begin,' sighed Lucy.

Just then Pete Grubb came back carrying Romula.

'What's all this I hear about 2.15 disappearing?'

'He's gone,' announced 3.45. 'He left this daft note.'

'Well 3.45,' said Pete Grubb nervously, 'he's been up in my spare room a lot lately and he asked me not to tell you about it. There may be a clue up there.'

'Take me there,' said 3.45 baring her teeth.

'I'll come too,' said Grandad hurriedly.

So the three of them set off. They were back a few minutes later.

'So what did you find?' asked Gran breathlessly.

'A *Teach Yourself Russian* course,' said Grandad.

'So that's it,' said Gran. 'Russia, of course. He's been to America which is one superpower and now he's gone off to the other. He's trying to persuade the leaders to help him to save the forests.'

'Yes,' agreed Lucy, 'that would tie in with the letter.'

'Russia,' growled 3.45, 'where is this Russia?'

Grandad got out his glasses and showed it to her on the map.

'Where is France?' she snapped.

'Here,' said Grandad, pointing to it.

'Ha,' said 3.45. 'So this Russia is much further away?'

'Yes,' said Grandad.

'So,' continued 3.45, 'he must be planning to go by plane. It's not near like France, he can't go quickly by boat.'

'That's right,' said Grandad. 'If we could alert all the airports that 2.15 is trying to get on a plane to Russia they might be able to intercept him.'

'That's what we must do,' declared Gran. 'He can't go running off all round the world. He'll get put in prison or something. We've got to stop him.'

'Lord Muxborough knows people in the government. Let's go and tell him,' added Pete Grubb.

They all crammed into Grandad's car and drove up to Muxborough Hall as fast as they could. As soon as they told Lord Muxborough what was happening, he phoned his friends in the Foreign Office and told them the story.

'Yes, that's right, 2.15, the wolf who visited the President of the United States. Yes, well the blighter has taken off to the Soviet Union. Yes you did hear right, Russia. Well quite, it could be dashed embarrassing for Her Majesty's Government. What do I suggest you do? Hang on a moment, I'll consult.'

'Tell them to watch all planes going to Russia and all ships and trains as well, just in case,' Gran told him.

'Right you are,' mumbled Lord Muxborough. After a while he put the phone down. 'Told them 2.15 might be disguised as a person or just as a dog, but either way they're watching all airports, stations and ports for him. They're confident he won't get past. They'll phone me as soon as anything happens. How can I get in touch with you, 3.45?'

'I'm very worried and I'm very cross,' said 3.45 looking troubled. 'Could I stay here with you and wait? Don't want to be entertained or anything, you can ignore me. Just want to be here if a call comes through.'

'Of course,' said Lord Muxborough. 'Pleasure and all that, don't you know. But I'd be a bit worried about the cubs, priceless antiques all around.'

'We'll take the cubs,' said Gran quickly.

So 3.45 stayed up at Muxborough Hall and got on rather well with the Muxboroughs. Every day Gran and Grandad and Lucy took the cubs up to visit her and every day there was no news.

' 'e's slipped through the net,' said Grandad. ' 'e's fooled us all.'

'Someone should go to Moscow and try to find him before he gets into too much trouble,' said Gran.

'Quite so,' agreed Lord Muxborough. 'The Foreign Office is very worried. They think there might be a diplomatic incident, after all I suppose 2.15 is British in a way, isn't he?'

'Not what the Consul in France said,' sniffed Grandad. ''e said 2.15 was a citizen of the world.'

'Well, yes,' said Lord Muxborough. 'But be that as it may, 2.15 does live here and the British Government might be held responsible if something unfortunate did happen. The British Ambassador in Moscow has been informed. But he can't do much because he wouldn't recognise 2.15 if he saw him.'

'I'd better go,' said Grandad. 'Breakin' a basic rule they taught me in the army, never volunteer for anything. Still 2.15's been a good mate to me and I fancy seein' Russia. I met some Russian soldiers at the end of the war, I'll look them up.'

'I can't go,' said Gran, '3.45 will need some help looking after the cubs.'

'Can I go with Grandad?' asked Lucy. 'I'm very worried about 2.15 and I do have a special relationship with him.'

It was agreed that Grandad and Lucy would take a plane the following day to Moscow. So Lucy went home and packed all her thick winter clothes and Mum and Dad took her round to Grandad's house. Grandad was all ready, wrapped up in a big coat and a scarf and hat pulled down firmly on his head.

'I'm a bit scared,' confessed Grandad. 'I've never been in a plane before.'

'Oh Grandpa Bert!' squeaked Romula. 'If you're going in an aeroplane, can I come too? Oh please, Grandpa Bert, I do so love aeroplanes.'

'Don't be silly, Romula,' snapped 3.45. 'Come here and be quiet.'

'Please find our Daddy and bring him back,' said Remus and Mowgli.

'Yes,' added 3.45 gruffly, 'and tell him I miss him.'

'Don't you worry, 3.45,' said Lucy giving her a big hug. 'We'll find him in no time and bring him back to you.'

'Thanks,' said 3.45 and gave Lucy a little peck. 'Never thought I'd do that,' she sniffed, 'kissing people indeed.'

Lucy and Grandad got into the car and everyone waved them goodbye. Lucy looked out of the back window and waved.

'Funny,' she commented to Grandad, 'there were only two cubs with 3.45.'

'I expect Romula went off to see her favourite Uncle Pete,' said Grandad.

At Moscow airport they went through passport control without any problems. Then they went into the customs shed. A big Russian opened Lucy's suitcase. He showed her a list of things she was not allowed to bring into the country.

'Do you have any of these?' he asked. Lucy shook her head. He rummaged through her suitcase.

'Ah,' he said smiling. 'You have brought a nice warm fur coat for your trip to Russia.'

'No,' said Lucy frowning. 'I don't have a fur . . .' Then she stopped and caught Grandad's eye.

'Come off it, Lucy,' he said. 'You've gone and forgotten all about that coat your Gran had cut down for you from that old beaver fur.'

'That's right,' said Lucy, her heart sinking, 'so I did.'

'Have a nice trip in Russia,' said the customs officer pleasantly. Outside the British Ambassador was waiting in an official car.

'So glad you could come,' he said shaking hands. 'This wolf business has got us in the most terrible tizz. You've no idea where he is?'

'No,' said Grandad, 'But I've got a pretty good idea where his daughter Romula is,' and he opened Lucy's case.

'Hello, Grandpa Bert,' said Romula cheerfully, sticking her head out from underneath Lucy's underwear.

'Oh,' said the Ambassador. 'Well, well, how sweet. She couldn't wait to see her Daddy.'

'Oh no, no,' said Romula, shaking her head. 'I just did so much want to go up in an aeroplane again.'

Grandad groaned. 'As if we didn't 'ave enough problems, now we've got a cub on our 'ands as well. I've a

108

good mind to give you a proper hiding, Romula.'

'I'll be very good, Grandpa Bert,' Romula assured him, 'and I will help you look for my Daddy.'

'You're very naughty,' Lucy told the cub.

'I know,' said Romula snuggling up to her, 'but I think you do like me anyway.'

The first thing they did when they got to the Embassy was to ring England to let 3.45 know that Romula was safe. Then they tried to decide what to do.

'Who do you both think 2.15 wants to see?' asked the Ambassador.

'Someone 'igh up in the government,' said Grandad.

'He'll have a hard time here,' said the Ambassador. 'Security is very tight in Russia.'

' 'e'll manage,' said Grandad proudly, ' 'ee's very re-sourceful is 2.15.'

'Yes indeed,' said the Ambassador, 'so it would seem. Now would you both like to have a shower and change? I thought maybe you would like to go and see some Russian dancing tonight. It's something visitors usually enjoy.'

'Super,' said Lucy.

'Why not?' agreed Grandad.

So that evening they went off leaving Romula asleep in front of the fire, with some hot milk and well guarded by two marines.

It was a rather grand theatre and they had very good seats.

A box near the stage was draped with Russian flags and there were plenty of troops on guard.

'Someone important is coming tonight,' said the Ambassador. 'I wonder who it is.'

Everyone stood up as they played the National Anthem. As the music finished a man came into the decorated box.

'My goodness,' whispered the Ambassador, 'it's the President himself.'

Then the lights went out and the dancing started. First of all there was a beautiful ballet with lots of girls in white dancing on their toes. Lucy loved it but Grandad dropped off. Then came a cossack dance with loud music and lots of clapping. Grandad sat up.

'This is more like it,' he whispered to Lucy.

Then on came dozens of men leaping across the stage wearing baggy trousers, high boots, white belted shirts and fur hats. Lucy was dazzled as they jumped and whirled faster and faster, kicking their legs out in front of them and leaping higher in the air than seemed possible. Suddenly Lucy began to giggle.

'Cut it out,' hissed Grandad.

'Look at that man over there,' whispered Lucy, 'he's let his fur hat come right down over his face, he can't see where he's going and his dancing is a bit odd too.'

'That's no man,' said Grandad, 'that's a wolf, that's 2.15.'

Grandad poked the Ambassador in the ribs and whispered: 'That dancer over there, the one with the 'at down over 'is 'ead, that's 2.15.'

'Good gracious!' exclaimed the Ambassador. 'We'd better go and warn the President before anything happens. Follow me.'

The Ambassador, Grandad and Lucy all pushed their way out, treading on people's toes and getting lots of irritated comments. They ran as fast as they could to the back of the theatre and just as they were about to go through the door that led to the boxes they saw 2.15 leap in the air and land in the Presidential box. They dashed through the door and raced up the stairs three at a time till they got to the box. Two huge policemen blocked the

110

entrance to the box. The Ambassador got his official papers out of his pocket. 'British Ambassador,' he told the guards in Russian. 'Got to see the President. Matter of great urgency. These are my friends.'

Under the watchful eye of the guards they were allowed in and there, all dressed in his cossack clothes, sat 2.15 shaking hands with the President. The performance had stopped and everyone was staring up at the box. The Ambassador bowed to the Head of State.

'Ah, the Ambassador from Britain,' cried the President. 'I see that the whole world wants to come into my box tonight.'

'Lucy, Grandad,' said 2.15. 'What a surprise, how did you get here?'

'I was just about to ask you the same question,' said Grandad.

'Will someone please explain to me what it is that is going on,' demanded the President.

'This wolf,' explained the Ambassador, 'is the wolf out of Red Riding Hood. He lives in a forest in Britain (though I hasten to add he is not a British citizen) and I think he wants to talk to you about matters of universal concern.'

'Ah,' said the President, smiling broadly. 'This is the wolf who appeared on the British television and then went to America. And now he comes to me. You are welcome Mr Wolf. Welcome to Russia.'

'Thank you, Mr President,' said 2.15. 'I never had any doubt that I would be welcome in your great country. You see,' he said to Lucy and Grandad, 'I told you that I would be treated as a friend everywhere.'

'Of course you are welcome in Russia,' said the President, 'for this is the land of wolves. Every Russian child is raised on that story and other stories of wolves too. To me you are no stranger but a childhood friend.'

'Good,' declared the wolf, grinning broadly. 'Now Comrade Leader, perhaps you could tell some of these soldiers to go away.'

They looked down and realised that soldiers with rifles pointing at 2.15 were standing all round the theatre. The President stood up:

'Good people,' he said. 'This wolf in my box is no enemy but an old friend of mine and of yours for he is none other than the wolf from *Red Riding Hood*.'

Murmers of disbelief ran round the theatre. The Ambassador took the chance to translate the President's speech for 2.15, Lucy and Grandad.

'And he has come all the way from the forest he lives in in England to bring a message to the Russian people. He has already visited the United States and been made welcome there; let us be sure he is given no less warm a welcome here. So let the performance continue. I will watch it with my friend the wolf and his comrades from England.'

When the performance was over, 2.15 walked with the President to his car. Crowds lined the pavement cheering. 2.15 smiled and waved.

'I hope you will do me the honour of staying at my residence,' said the President.

'He can't do that,' said Grandad firmly, ' 'is daughter smuggled herself into the country and is waiting for 'im at the Embassy under armed guard.'

'Romula,' cried 2.15 laughing. 'Oh dear, she really is a chip off the old block. Take me to her without delay.'

So it was agreed that 2.15 would stay with the Ambassador and would visit the Head of State in the Kremlin the next day. 2.15 and the others rushed back to the Embassy as fast as they could. Romula leapt into her father's arms.

'Daddy, I did go in an aeroplane again.'

'You're a very naughty little cub,' 2.15 told her. 'Now come on, let's phone Mummy together and let her know we're all right.'

So 2.15 phoned Lord Muxborough's number.

'Hello, my love,' he cried. 'Everything has gone according to plan. Tomorrow I shall ask for help in saving the world's forests and then I shall come straight home to my favourite wolf.'

There was a silence and 2.15 held the phone away and looked at it.

'She's hung up on me. I expect she's just a tiny bit cross.'

'Don't know what you expect,' declared Grandad. 'You go off leaving her a silly note, worry the poor wolf to death. It's no wonder she gets cross.'

'I know, I know,' admitted 2.15. 'But I have to try and save the forests.'

'How did you get out of the country?' demanded Lucy. 'All the airports and ports were watched.'

'I knew they would be,' said 2.15, 'so I took a fishing boat to Norway and then I met some Arctic wolves and explained to them what was happening and I ran with them right across Northern Norway and Sweden and Finland till I came to Russia. Then I found my way to Moscow and pretended to be a dog until I found a way to get to see the President. Dead easy.'

'You just ran over all those countries?' asked Lucy dubiously.

'Of course,' replied the wolf. 'Wolves are sensible, no frontiers, no passports, no visas for them, just space and running, it's wonderful. I loved it. But I had my mission to fulfil so I came here as quickly as I could. The Head of State says I can be on television very soon, to tell the people all about acid rain and things. Then we can return to our own dear forest.'

'You were very lucky to get away with it, 2.15,' said Grandad, 'you could have been in dead trouble.'

'I know,' agreed the wolf, 'but I had to do it. So much is at stake.'

Two days later 2.15 was on television once again with Romula on his knee, telling the Russian people about the world's forests and the danger they were in and asking for their support. Romula added in her high pitched voice:

'Please help us save my nice home and all the forests 'cos that would be good for all the people and all the animals.'

The next day they made their way to Moscow airport to catch the plane home.

'Another trip on an aeroplane,' squeaked Romula with delight.

As they walked through the airport lots of people came up to 2.15 to shake his paw. They spoke in Russian and 2.15 couldn't understand any of it but he shook their hands and hugged them and smiled.

'They're all saying how much they enjoyed your television speech,' the Ambassador told him. 'And they're wishing you luck.'

'You see,' said 2.15, 'I was right, people do care about the forests, they care all over the world. Something will be done.'

10

The Wolf Walk

When Grandad, Lucy, 2.15 and Romula returned to London, they were met by hoards of journalists and television reporters. 2.15 gave them all the information they wanted. Gran and Lord Muxborough were waiting for them at the exit. Standing next to them, 2.15 spotted his old friend the Head of the Metropolitan Police.

'Hello,' cried the wolf cheerfully, 'we've just come back from Moscow.'

'Yes I know,' said the police chief sombrely. 'And I'm afraid I'll have to ask you to come with me, 2.15. As you're a British resident I'm afraid I'm going to have to ask you some questions about your trip.'

'Ask away,' said the wolf.

'Well, not here,' said the Chief of Police. 'I'm sorry about this, 2.15, but you're under arrest again.'

'Come, come, come,' said 2.15 laughing. 'That's not possible. I have been spreading the message about saving the forests. No one could object to that.'

'Some people do,' said the Police Chief. 'And quite important people too. My instructions are to take you in for questioning and to stop you from gallivanting all over the world. You could cause a serious diplomatic incident.'

'Nonsense,' said the wolf. 'Let your spirit be at peace on this issue, I shall do nothing but good.'

'You don't understand,' replied the Police Chief wearily, 'this has nothing to do with me. My instructions are to take you into Scotland Yard and wait there for further instructions.'

'You'll excuse me,' said 2.15, 'but I think I shall refuse your invitation.' With a huge leap he cleared the barrier and raced through the crowds of people.

'Stop that wolf!' yelled the Police Chief, but it was too late. 2.15 had disappeared from view.

'My Daddy,' cried Romula, 'my Daddy has run away.'

'Do any of you know where 2.15 might go?' asked the Police Chief.

'No,' said Grandad, 'most of his close friends in London 'ave moved away.'

'You're being very mean to poor 2.15,' said Lucy indignantly. 'After all the good he has done.'

'I don't like it either,' said the Police Chief. 'But people in high places feel uneasy about him.'

'You'll never find him,' said Lucy hotly. 'You won't even know what you're looking for, a person or a dog.'

Meanwhile 2.15 raced out of the airport and ran down into the underground and pretended to be a dog.

Later, when Lucy and Grandad were safely back in the forest, they sat in a sad little group round Gran's kitchen table.

'I do 'ope 'e 'as the sense to phone 'ere,' said Grandad. 'I want to warn 'im not to go near 'is old mates on the Isle of Dogs. The police are sure to look for 'im round there.'

'He'll think of that,' Gran assured him. 'But poor old wolf, he doesn't have anywhere else to go.'

'I'm sure he'll manage very well,' said Lucy. 'If there's one thing 2.15 is good at it's making friends.'

Just then the phone rang. Gran grabbed it.

'It's me, 2.15,' came the voice. 'I've only got 10 pence so I'll be brief. Tell 3.45 not to worry and I'll be back as soon as I can. Love to all . . .' Grandad grabbed the phone.

' 'Arf the police in Britain are looking for you, 2.15,' he said urgently. 'Lie low for a while.' Then the bips came.

'He didn't have time to say where he was,' said Grandad, 'but he sounded all right.'

'I'm going to give 2.15's message to 3.45,' said Lucy.

'No need,' came a voice and there was 3.45 jumping in through the window, followed by the three cubs. 'Romula says they tried to arrest 2.15.'

'They did,' said Grandad, 'and he's run off and is somewhere in London but is trying to get back here.'

'Did they want to lock him up?' asked 3.45.

'Probably,' said Grandad.

'Then he was right to run away,' said 3.45. 'People shouldn't lock wolves up. We don't like it.'

'As soon as 'e gets back 'ere you should all disappear into the forest for a while,' said Grandad.

'It would be a pleasure,' growled 3.45. 'Come on, cubs. We've got to go into the forest and wait for Daddy.'

'We'll let you know the minute there's any news,' promised Gran, 'good or bad.'

In fact 2.15 had wandered round the streets of London feeling very lonely. He wandered round and round trying to think of a way to get out of the situation. Whenever 2.15 saw a policeman he hid somewhere. On the second day 2.15 came round a corner into a particularly run-down area and saw a policeman coming towards him. The wolf looked around for somewhere to hide and noticed that behind some dustbins there were some steps leading down to a basement. He ran down the steps as fast as he could and pressed against the door of the basement. The door gave way and he fell in. 2.15 looked around to see where he had landed. He was in a large room, which was empty

118

except for a couple of drums, a piano, a guitar and four young black men.

'It's a dog,' said one of them. 'Nothing to worry about. Come here boy, nice dog.'

2.15 cleared his throat: 'No sir, I am not a dog but a wolf. Now pray pardon me for breaking in on you like this, but I am endeavouring to avoid being apprehended by the police.'

'Hey, man, this wolf, he's the one who was on television – you know, going on about the destruction of the environment and that.'

'Yeh,' said another, 'I saw that, it was great. We're right behind you, it's evil what some people are doing to the planet.'

'You bring great joy to my sad heart,' cried the wolf. 'Whenever I meet ordinary people I get so much support.'

'But why are the police looking for you?'

'Because I recently made a trip to Moscow to put my

case about the forest,' 2.15 explained, 'and they want to lock me up in case I go off somewhere else and cause a diplomatic incident.'

'You went to Russia! Fantastic! Don't you worry, we'll look after you. We'll see you don't get put away.'

'You are indeed most kind,' said the wolf. 'Please let me introduce myself, I am 2.15.'

'Yeh, I know, out of Red Riding Hood. Great to meet you. I'm Winston, I'm the drummer; these are the others in our group, Eddie, Lionel and Mac.'

'Gentlemen, the pleasure is entirely mine. Now I don't wish to cause you any trouble or put you in any danger, but if I could just stay here for a short while I'd be very grateful.'

Eddie, Lionel and Mac had to go off and left 2.15 with Winston.

'Get in touch,' they said as they left. 'If you need any help at all, anything, just let us know.'

'Thanks,' said 2.15. 'It's good to be among friends again.'

'I'll just go home and get you a bit of nosh and a cushion,' said Winston.

'Splendid!' said 2.15. 'If you could remember please that I am a vegetarian and if you could manage a radio, I would be in paradise.'

Soon Winston returned with a large, cheerful looking woman.

'2.15, this is my Mum. She insisted on meeting you.'

'How do you do, 2.15. I'm Mrs McLeod, Winston's mother. I had to meet you because I just love the story of Red Riding Hood. My mother used to tell it to me and I told it to my children. Isn't that so, Winston?'

'Right on, Mum.'

'So when Winston told me you were here, I made up

120

some nice vegetable soup and brought it over with some bread. Here it is, all nice and warm. And I want you to know if you need something, you just say so. I think it's a crying shame, you doing so much good and they want to put you away. I mean you've got all those children to bring up. It was all on the news, you know. I brought a radio, so you can listen.'

While 2.15 drank the soup they listened to the news. In it 2.15 was described as a grey wolf, rather dog-like in appearance.

'Hey, Mum,' yelled Winston. 'I've got an idea. Why don't we get Donna to dye 2.15's coat brown. They won't be looking for a brown wolf. She's my girlfriend, she's a hairdresser.'

'That is one hell of a good idea,' said Winston's Mum.

'I don't wish to appear ungrateful,' said 2.15, 'but I am a little wary of hairdressers and the like. I was once taken to an establishment called Pampered Pets where my coat was shaved off and then, the crowning indignity, they put a bow on me.'

'You don't have to worry about anything like that with Donna,' said Winston's Mum. 'She's a very sensible girl and she'll support you in your stand. She's always going on marches about whales and rain forests and endangered species and that. She'll just change the colour of your coat.'

'But I like being dark grey,' said 2.15. 'It's my colour. I wouldn't feel like me if I was dark brown. 3.45 and all the cubs are dark grey. It's a beautiful colour.'

'Right on, man,' agreed Winston, 'black and dark grey are beautiful.'

'That is not the point, son,' said Mrs McLeod. 'Remember the police are looking for a grey wolf. Now come on, 2.15, if you let Donna make you a nice brown, you can

121

come and live in our flat all nice and warm and lots of company. No one will be looking for a brown dog. We can say we just got ourselves a dog. Come on, what do you say?'

'I'll do it,' cried 2.15. 'Madam, to live in your home no sacrifice would be too great. Let the fair Donna be summoned.'

'We'll have to take 2.15 to the flat, Mum,' said Winston. 'If she's going to dye him, he'll have to go in the bath.'

Late that night 2.15 was smuggled into Winston's flat. A little later Donna turned up. She walked up to 2.15 and shook his hand.

'It's a real thrill to meet you,' she said enthusiastically. 'I watched you on the TV and you were just brilliant. I kept thinking, maybe they'll listen to a wolf.'

'Madam,' replied 2.15, kissing her hand gallantly, 'if my simple words had such a profound effect on you then my efforts have not been in vain.'

'Winston says the police are after you.'

'Alas, yes, that is indeed the case, they fear I may cause a diplomatic incident and want me safely locked away.'

'Don't you worry, 2.15. By the time I've finished with you your own mother wouldn't recognise you. Now look at this colour chart. What do you fancy, auburn glow or burned chestnut?'

2.15 groaned. '3.45 isn't going to like this one bit.'

'She'll like it a whole lot better than having you locked up,' pointed out Winston's Mum. 'Come on now, choose.'

'As always madam, pearls of wisdom fall from your lips. I shall have this one, I think, tawny brown.'

'It's a bit dull,' commented Donna. 'Could I give you some highlights to liven it up, you'd look really good.'

'Donna,' said 2.15 firmly, 'much as I appreciate your

efforts on my behalf, the memory of my humiliation at Pampered Pets is still in the forefront of my memory. Pray do something simple and uncomplicated.'

So 2.15 was put in the bath and Donna rubbed the tawny brown into his coat and after many rinsings 2.15's fur was blown dry.

'It's worked!' cried Donna. 'It's great, who would recognise him.'

'It's fantastic, man,' said Winston.

'You've done good,' said Winston's Mum. 'He looks like a mongrel now.'

'Something tells me I'm not going to like what I see. But lead me to a mirror,' said 2.15 diffidently.

He looked at his reflection for a few moments: 'Hum, it works very well as camouflage but I truly dread to think what 3.45 will have to say.'

'Don't you go worrying yourself over that,' said Winston's Mum. 'She'll be so relieved to have you back in one piece she won't say nothing.'

'You don't know 3.45,' 2.15 told her. 'Madam, I am exhausted from all this. Could I trouble you for a cup of tea?'

They all sat round drinking tea and waiting for the next news bulletin. 2.15 asked Donna if she didn't find dying hair a bit boring.

'Oh, it is,' she told him. 'I mean, it's a job, but what I'd really like to do is go to college and study philosophy.'

'A wonderful idea!' cried the wolf. 'I myself would like to do that.'

'Yeh,' agreed Donna, 'it's fascinating.'

'Then why don't you do it?' asked the wolf.

'Because I have to earn money to help my Mum out,' Donna told him.

'I see, I see,' said 2.15. 'Money again, it so often is the

123

stumbling block, but one I have found quite easy to combat.'

'How?' demanded Donna.

'I used to do an Amazing Performing Dog Show with my friend Lucy but I can't do that now. Let me think of something else. What can I do to help?'

'You couldn't raise that amount of money,' said Donna, 'but thanks for the thought, 2.15.'

'Hang on, Donna,' interrupted Winston. 'What about the dance contest. Maybe 2.15 would have some ideas on that.'

'A dance contest?' enquired 2.15. 'People do do the oddest things. What is it?'

'It's a competition for a new dance. The prize money is amazing, it's £5,000. Donna and I are going in for it. We've been practising a new dance for months. It's O.K. but it's not great. I wouldn't rate our chances very high.'

'A new dance,' mused 2.15. 'Huumm, well it has always offended me that there is a foxtrot but no dance called after a wolf. I mean wolves and foxes have a lot in common, both of us being frequently mentioned in fairy stories and usually in an unflattering light. Why should foxes have something wolves don't, I ask myself. Now I would suggest a new dance called the wolf walk.'

'But, 2.15, the foxtrot is dead old-fashioned. It's not that sort of dance we're thinking of. We need something, you know, modern and zappy.'

'And you shall have it, never fear. Come on, push back the furniture and let's get going.'

When a space was cleared 2.15 walked up and down and clicked his feet in the air and pranced in a variety of wolfish ways.

'Come on now, you two,' said Winston's Mum, 'see what you two can do with that.'

So Donna and Winston began to work out a routine. Every so often 2.15 would demonstrate the wolf walk again until Donna and Winston had a really exciting rhythm and sequence.

'It looks really good,' said Winston's Mum. 'I'm going to put on a record and then I'm going to have a go myself because I don't see why you young things should have all the fun.'

'Madam,' said 2.15. 'May I have the honour?'

And the four of them danced round the room laughing and having a whale of a time.

When the evening of the competition came round, Winston and Donna paraded in the best finery.

'Donna, you look as pretty as a picture,' said Winston's Mum.

'Yes indeed,' cried 2.15. 'Like the princess in a fairy tale, and Winston, you are a snazzy dresser man, you look terrific, both of you. Now off you go and win. A lot is at stake. Donna you could go to university and Winston you could have your own photography studio, and more than that the honour of the wolf walk is on the line. So be off, the two of you, and show 'em the superiority of the wolf walk over all other dances.'

2.15 and Winston's Mum sat down and tried to watch TV, but neither of them could concentrate. They played cards and drank a bottle of wine but both of them were too anxious to enjoy anything. Suddenly 2.15 called out: 'There's a taxi drawing up outside. They're getting out. He's holding his hands up like a boxer. They've won. They've won!'

'Well, praise the Lord,' said Winston's Mum. 'It's so wonderful, 2.15. Now the two of them will have a chance in life.'

'Madam, I might almost dare to hope that they will live happily ever after.'

Winston and Donna were so excited they could hardly talk. But they told 2.15 they'd already decided what to do with the money.

'We're going to give our parents a trip home to the West Indies,' Donna told him. 'And then we'll split the rest, except for a cheque to the Wildlife Fund as a special thank you to you, 2.15.'

2.15 looked sad. 'What's up?' asked Winston. 'Aren't you pleased we won?'

'Yes of course, I'm delighted,' replied the wolf, 'absolutely delighted, but the mention of the Wildlife Fund reminded me of my mission and my situation. And while you good people could not have been kinder I need to run around freely again. No offence meant, but I do feel cooped up here.'

'Let's give this some thought,' said Donna. 'Between us

we must be able to come up with something.'

'Maybe one of you could contact my friend Sir Samuel Wolf. I don't dare go and see him myself. I suspect his home and his office are being watched. But one of you could ring him and leave a rather obscure message,' mused the wolf.

'I'll do that for you with pleasure,' said Winston.

'Then we should get Sir Samuel to an unlikely place where I could speak with him, Wolf to wolf.'

'I've got an idea,' said Winston. '2.15, would you mind being disguised.'

'Dressing up, you mean? Oh no, I love to change identities and play with disguises. Oh, it sounds like good fun, Winston, I'll go along with that. Something to look forward to.'

The next day Winston rang Sir Samuel Wolf: 'It's very urgent. It's regarding the welfare of an – eh– relative of his, a Mr eh, T.F. Wolf.'

'One moment, please,' said the secretary. 'Yes, Sir Samuel will speak to you now. Putting you through.'

'Hello, this is Sir Samuel Wolf. I understand you have some news of my cousin, Mr T.F. Wolf.'

'Yes, that is correct. If you could meet me under the Queen Elizabeth Hall on the South Bank tonight, I might be able to help you contact Mr T.F. Wolf.'

'I'll be there at about 8 o'clock.'

So that evening Winston said to 2.15:

'You know you wanted some exercise. Well I'm going skateboarding. Would you like to give it a whirl?'

'I don't know what it is,' said the wolf.

'Oh, it's great man, really great. But a dog skateboarding might attract attention, so I borrowed a friend's gear. I thought you could dress up as a Rastafarian.'

'Dread man, dread,' said 2.15. 'I would like that.'

127

'Great, well here's the gear and Donna got you an old wig from her work.'

So 2.15 dressed up in the wig and wore dark glasses and some very elegant clothes.

He admired himself in the mirror. 'I look good, mighty cool. I like this image. Of all my disguises, I like this one the best.'

They drove to the Queen Elizabeth Hall and went to the area under the hall where groups of young men were leaping and jumping on skateboards. 2.15 watched with wide eyes.

'They're brilliant,' he gasped, 'brilliant. How do they do it?'

The group continued to whirl and twist and run up the side of the building, jump in the air and land on their feet. 2.15's eyes glowed.

'It looks like the most splendid fun,' he cried. 'Let me attempt these athletic feats.'

So all evening 2.15 jumped around: 'It's great,' he yelled to Winston. 'I haven't had so much fun for years.'

Suddenly Sir Samuel turned up and looked around at the skateboarders but saw no one who he even vaguely recognised.

2.15 spotted him: 'Hi there. Come and have a go on my skateboard.'

'Are you the young man who phoned me earlier today about my friend Mr T.F. Wolf?' demanded Sir Samuel.

'No, it's me, don't you recognise me, it's me, 2.15.'

'I should have known it,' said Sir Samuel. 'It is the most wonderful disguise. The best yet. I wouldn't have known you in a million years.'

'Not only the best,' cried 2.15, 'but the most fun. Here, you have a go.'

'2.15, be serious, the police are looking for you. We've

got to get you out of London as soon as possible. Now wait here. Taffy Evans is parked just round the corner with a van full of vegetables. We'll put you in the truck and cover you with carrots and leeks and get you back to the forest as quickly as we can.'

'Back to my beloved 3.45.'

'Just so and you're to stay in the forest and do nothing, absolutely nothing to draw attention to yourself, do you understand that 2.15?'

'Dear friend, lead me on to the spuds and the cabbages,' declared 2.15. 'Nothing will keep me from my 3.45. Skateboarders, it has been a great, great pleasure to be one of your number. Farewell.'

11

Auld Lang Syne

When 2.15 finally returned from London, he disappeared into the forest and no one saw him for over a week. On Boxing Day Gran and Grandad and Lucy were driving over to Lord Muxborough's for a drink when they heard the horns of the hunt.

'Huh,' commented Grandad sourly. 'That lot 'ave got nothin' better to do with their time than go around chasin' them poor little foxes.'

'It must be really awful to be a fox,' commented Lucy sadly.

Suddenly a streak of browny-grey flashed by the car.

'Yoiks and tally ho!' it cried and waved and dashed off into a field.

'That wasn't no fox,' said Grandad. 'That was 2.15.'

They stopped the car and moments later the hounds of the hunt ran panting across the road followed by a red clad rider on horseback.

'Grandad,' cried Lucy, 'we've got to find 2.15 before the dogs get him. They'll tear poor 2.15 to bits, because they'll think he's a fox,' and tears poured down her cheeks.

'Don't fret, love,' said Grandad. 'We'll head him off down by the ford.'

Grandad turned the car round and raced through fields at seventy miles an hour. When they got to the ford, Lucy and Grandad got out of the car and ran towards a clearing where they could hear the dogs barking. As they stumbled along, the sound of the dogs gradually died away.

'Come on, Grandad,' urged Lucy. 'The dogs must have got him. We may be too late.'

Suddenly they found themselves in a clearing. In the middle sat 2.15 on a tree stump barking at the dogs.

'Oh 2.15,' panted Lucy, 'we were so worried. We thought the dogs had got you.'

'Dear friends,' cried the wolf standing up and helping Grandad over to the stump. 'Come and sit down. You are quite tired out. You need not have feared for my well being. I have decided to put a stop to this cruel and unnatural sport in this area. So I substituted myself for the poor little foxy. Now if you'll excuse me I've got these villainous dogs to deal with,' and he barked at the hounds again. He barked and barked in an angry tone.

'Woof, woof-woof-woof, WOOF, WOOF, WOOF.'

The dogs hung their heads, sat down and sniffed and whimpered.

'What are you saying to them, 2.15?' asked Lucy.

'I'm telling them they should be ashamed, chasing that fox just for fun, and that animals should stick together and that the fox was some vixen's much loved cub and how would they feel if a pack of foxes chased their little ones like that?'

The circle of dogs began to cry.

'And another thing,' said 2.15, 'woof, woof.'

One of the dogs let out a small bark.

'That's no excuse,' said 2.15, 'no excuse at all.'

At that moment the hunt rode up and, seeing the extraordinary scene, the huntsmen dismounted and looked at the dogs in dismay.

'I say,' said the leader of the hunt, 'what's going on here?'

'What is going on is that these dogs have seen the error of their ways and have promised never to chase poor little foxes again,' said 2.15.

'Piffle,' shouted the master of the hunt. 'Piffle and poppycock. And who are you, anyway?'

'The name, sir, is 2.15 and I am the wolf out of Red Riding Hood. I have quite recently given up the grannie eating business and am now a happily married wolf and the proud father of three. Now, I have a certain fellow feeling for foxes. They also appear in many stories and, like wolves, often in an unfavourable light. I cannot bear to think of any fellow creature, also beloved of its mother and father, being destroyed in this barbarous way.'

'Piffle and poppycock,' said the master again. 'The fox enjoys it.'

'That is not my impression from my dealings with foxes,' said 2.15 sternly. 'Now, sir, I urge you to forswear this cruel sport, just as these dogs have done under the spell of my oratory.'

'They've what?' demanded the master. 'I'll get another set of hounds.'

'No point,' said 2.15 smiling broadly, 'the same thing would only happen again. No sir, you will either have to give up the hunt or go and live elsewhere. In the vicinity of 2.15's forest there will be no foxhunting.'

'We'll see about that,' snarled the master. 'Unless I'm much mistaken you're the wolf the police are looking for. We don't need the likes of you telling us what to do.' And he rode away followed by the other members of the hunt. The dogs slunk after them barking at 2.15 over their shoulders. 2.15 waved and gave them the thumbs up sign.

'What are they saying?' asked Lucy.

'Only that I'm not to worry, they won't go back on their word,' the wolf told her. 'Now that's what I call a good morning's work.'

'I think you're barmy, that's what I think,' said Grandad. 'You're supposed to be lying low and you've just announced to the whole neighbourhood that you're back in the forest.'

'But I had to save the poor little foxes,' explained 2.15. 'You would not have me be cruel and heartless.'

'No,' said Grandad, 'just sensible.'

Soon afterwards a policeman turned up at Muxborough Hall.

'Sorry to bother you, sir,' he said to Lord Muxborough,

'particularly in the festive season, but we've had substantiated reports that the wolf is back in these parts. Interfering with the Boxing Day hunt, he was.'

'Well, eh, yes Constable, I heard about that. Rum stuff eh?'

'Personally sir, I don't hold with fox hunting and I agree with what he has to say about the environment and that. But the fact is there's a warrant out for his arrest.'

'Quite so, officer, quite so, but I honestly don't know where he is, gone running off into the forest somewhere.'

'Well, sir, I'll have to report to London that he's been seen round here. Whatever my personal feelings in the case, I have my duty to do.'

'Quite so, Constable, I feel conflicting loyalties myself. 2.15 is very intelligent and he understands these things. I don't think he'll be in touch with any of his friends round here. Considerate sort of wolf you know, wouldn't want to put anyone on the spot.'

Later that afternoon there was a gathering at Gran and Grandad's house. Grandad had made some mince pies and all 2.15's friends in the village sat round and tried to decide what to do next.

'We can't 'and 'im over,' said Grandad, 'that much is clear.'

'But the law is the law, Bert,' pointed out Pete Grubb.

'We're in a dilemma,' agreed Lord Muxborough. 'None of us wants to break the law and none of us wants to help put poor old 2.15 behind bars.'

'The best thing would be if 2.15 and his family could simply disappear for a while,' said Grandad sadly.

'I wouldn't 'arf miss 'im,' said Grandad.

'Quite so,' said Lady Muxborough, 'I'd be devastated, heartbroken, I mean he's such a sweetie and I've even become fond of 3.45 and those terrible cubs. But I agree,

I think the safest solution would be for them to vanish.'

'Lucy,' said Gran, 'you know 2.15 better than any one of us and you're the one he's closest to. You go into the forest and see if you can find 2.15 and tell him what we've decided and why. He'll understand.'

'All right,' said Lucy, trying not to cry, 'for his own good I'll go.'

She put on her red anorak, took a basket full of mince pies and went off into the forest.

'2.15,' she called out. 'Where are you. Please come out, it's important.'

'Ah ha, Red Riding Hood, I smell goodies in your basket. Are you going to let me have a peep and see what delicacies you have in there?'

'Oh 2.15, what a relief, I am pleased to see you. Here are some mince pies for you and the family because it's Christmas. Grandad cooked them.'

'Bet he was glad of a change from apple pie,' said 2.15 grinning and he munched one of the mince pies. 'Umm, yummy, I love Grandad's pastry. Now what's so important?'

'Oh 2.15, it's dreadful. When the police in London know you're in the forest they'll come looking for you. We've been having a meeting and we all feel that for your own safety, you and 3.45 and the cubs should disappear for a while.'

'I see,' said the wolf. 'Well, by some odd chance I had a similar discussion this very day with my beloved 3.45 and we have decided to leave the forest and go and live in Fairy Tale Land with the babes.'

'Not for ever, 2.15?' asked Lucy, her eyes filling with tears.

'I think so, Lucy, my love. The world is such a dangerous place, I feel my cubs would be better off in the magic lands of the Fairy Tales.'

'Oh 2.15, if you go away for ever, who'll speak out for the forest and the rivers and the seas and the threatened species of animals?'

'You Lucy, you. You must take on the responsibility.'

'But 2.15, I'm only a child.'

'Yes, but the world is full of children, hundreds of thousands of millions of you. You must take care of the world, it is a wonderful place and it deserves loving care. You, the children, must insist that the world continues to be a beautiful place to live in.'

'I'll try 2.15, I'll try, I promise I'll try but I'll miss you so much.'

'I'll miss you too, Lucy, my Little Red Riding Hood, who wasn't. Now don't cry and ask Lord Muxborough to be kind enough to give a New Year's Eve Party and invite everyone on this list, for I want to leave my forest on a high note. I want a splendid party attended by my many human friends and I want it to be a happy occasion full of merriment and laughter, no tears. An evening people and wolves will remember with pleasure all the days of their lives.'

Lucy took the list and hugged 2.15 and returned to Gran and Grandad's, where everyone was waiting on tenterhooks.

'He's going back to Fairyland for ever,' Lucy told them. 'He thinks it will be safer for the cubs. And he says we're not to be miserable and he wants a big farewell party at Muxborough Hall on New Year's Eve, and here's the list of people he wants invited.'

Lord Muxborough took the list and looked down it: 'It's a long list but by jove it will be the best party ever. I'll have to ring round and invite people, it's too late to write. But we'll open up the ballroom at Muxborough Hall for the first time in ages and I guarantee that we'll all have the time of our lives.'

All the people on the list were phoned and all agreed to come, even if it meant cancelling something else.

'Mr Al-u-Din is providing the food,' Lady Muxborough told Lucy, 'Winston is bringing a steel band for the music, François Perrier or Gaston Loup or whatever his name is, is loading up his car with the best French Champagne – oh it's all going to be the most splendid fun. You know, my dear, before we met 2.15 we only knew one kind of person, landowners like ourselves, and now it's all such a romp, people come from all over the place and it's so much more interesting. I haven't had so much fun since I drove an ambulance during the war.'

'There's always fun around 2.15,' Lucy agreed. 'Look, I've made a special invitation for 2.15 and his family and I'm going to nail it to a tree in the forest, he's bound to find it.'

TO THE GREATEST WOLF IN THE WORLD AND HIS FAMILY. ALL YOUR MANY FRIENDS EXPECT YOU AT THE PARTY AT MUXBOROUGH HALL ON NEW YEAR'S EVE. DO COME AND NO NEED TO BRING A BOTTLE – LITTLE RED RIDING HOOD AND GRANNIE.

'He'll like that,' said Lady Muxborough, 'particularly the greatest wolf bit.'

'It's true,' said Lucy, 'he is.'

Everything went according to plan and on the day of New Year's Eve everyone was busy decorating the ballroom of Muxborough Hall, laying the tables, polishing glasses and arranging flowers. In the middle of all the preparations there was a ring at the front door.

'Probably Pete Grubb with extra plates,' said Gran. 'I'll go and let him in.'

A moment later she returned looking grave:

'It's the Chief Commissioner of the Metropolitan Police,' she said, 'and he wants to talk to you, Muffy.'

'Oh dear,' sighed Lord Muxborough descending a ladder, 'and we so nearly made it. Oh well, have to talk to the fellow I suppose.'

So Lord Muxborough took the Chief Commissioner into his library.

'Sorry to intrude, Lord Muxborough, when you're obviously about to celebrate the New Year in some style.'

'Not to worry. Please be seated. Now what can I do for you?'

'Frankly, Lord Muxborough, I was wondering if this party might have something to do with 2.15 returning from his foreign gallivantings? I know how much he's done for you and Muxborough Hall but 2.15 is wanted by the police and it's your duty to tell me what you know.'

'Oh dear,' sighed Lord Muxborough, 'I knew it would come to this. To be perfectly straight with you, this is a farewell party for 2.15 and his family, as they are leaving us for good.'

'Well I'll be blowed!' said the policeman. 'Where are they going?'

'Back to Fairy Land, I understand. 2.15 feels the world is a dangerous place and that the cubs will have a better chance there.'

'I see. Well to be perfectly honest with you, Muxborough, I'm delighted. I really like 2.15 and just between the two of us I agree with what he's been trying to do. I'd have hated to put him in prison. Childhood friend of mine too you know.'

'So you won't arrest him?'

138

'Good heavens no! We want him out of the way. From our point of view this is the best solution. I wonder if I could stay and say goodbye to him and wish him luck. Only met him twice but I did find him a very decent sort of a chap, eh wolf.'

'Delighted, old chap, stay and join in the fun by all means.'

As the evening wore on people poured into Muxborough Hall. 2.15's London friends, the families from the flats, Liz Howes, Mr Al-u-Din and family, the lads and their wives and children and the dogs who had been rescued, Sir Samuel and Lady Wolf, François and Arlette Perrier from France, Winston with his steel band, his Mum and Donna. In addition the whole population of the village turned up, including the Reverend Bell and Margaret Higgins and Andrew Compton and of course Gran and Grandad, Lucy and her parents and Pete and Lily Grubb.

At about 9 o'clock, 2.15 and his family arrived. As they entered the steel band stopped playing.

'2.15,' said Winston, 'we have written a calypso in your honour, and we'd like to play it for you: "The 2.15 Calypso." '

Gran and Grandad live in a high flat,
Along come 2.15 and he change all of that.
Him work very hard to earn lots of money.
And now they live in the country.

Oh 3.45 she live in the zoo,
That something she like not to do.
So 2.15 get the lads to get her out,
And now she do what she like and run all about.

Then 2.15 meet Sir Samuel,
He got lots of money but he not live so well,
Now he happy with his good wife,
And both of them having the time of their life.

2.15 met Mr Al-u-Din,
And became good friends with him.
2.15 help bring over his wife,
And now he got children and plenty of strife.

Lots of dogs in captivity,
2.15 think they should have liberty,
So he find them all a good home,
And now they have fun and they freely roam.

2.15 he become a dad,
Mowgli, Remus and Romula he had.
3.45 help him a little bit,
And the triplets them make quite a hit.

Muxborough Hall in a terrible way,
Till 2.15 him have his say.
Now it looks all glowing and clean,
And the tourists come in a steady stream.

2.15 get concerned about pollution,
Go and talk to the politician,
They try to shut him up and put him away,
But everyone agree with what he have to say.

2.15 meet Winston for a little talk,
Soon them work out the great wolf walk.
So Donna she going to university,
And Winston well he be mighty busy.

We all sorry that he's got to go.
But accept that it is so.
We feel so unhappy,
But we wish him luck and his family.

'Dear friends,' cried 2.15, 'I am overwhelmed by the love and affection you have shown and the numbers in which you have turned out. I don't need to tell you that I'm heartbroken at the prospect of leaving you but I felt the time had come to put 3.45 and the cubs first. Immediately after midnight the five of us will leave here and run out of your lives for ever. However I hope to live on, not only in the story of Red Riding Hood, but in the memories of those who knew me. I know that my concern for the future of the world's forests will be carried on by millions of people all over the world. Now enough talk, I want this to be a happy occasion, everyone is to have the time of their lives for the next three hours.

So Donna and Winston demonstrated the wolf walk and then everyone paired off to have a go. Lord Muxborough danced with Mrs Al-u-Din, Sir Samuel with Winston's Mum, François Perrier/Gaston Loup with Liz Howes, Pete Grubb danced with Romula, and Grandad persuaded 3.45 to dance with him.

'Who are you going to dance with, 2.15?' asked Winston, who was partnering Lady Muxborough.

'With my Little Red Riding Hood of course,' replied

the wolf. 'My first and dearest friend. Lucy, may I have the honour and pleasure of this dance?'

They all danced and laughed and ate and drank late into the night.

At 11.55 Lord Muxborough called out: 'Friends, make a circle, in five minutes it will be the New Year. Hold hands and let us greet the New Year with "Auld Lang Syne", and as we are about to say farewell to dear, dear friends this song will have a special meaning and sadness for all of us.'

So they made a circle and began to sing:

> *Lest auld acquaintance be forgot,*
> *And never called to mind.*
> *We'll drink a cup of friendship here,*
> *For the sake of auld lang syne.*
> *For auld lang syne, my friends,*
> *For auld lang syne,*
> *We'll drink a cup of kindness yet,*
> *For the sake of auld lang syne.*

'Happy New Year,' they shouted as the clocks struck twelve and everyone kissed everyone. Quickly glasses were filled.

'To 2.15 and 'is family, good luck and God bless 'em,' toasted Grandad.

The five wolves moved towards the door. 2.15's eyes were full of tears. He shook Grandad's hand and kissed Gran and Lucy, waved at the others and followed by his family ran out into the woods. The guests trooped out of Muxborough Hall and watched as the wolves disappeared out of sight among the trees.

'Uncle Pete,' came Romula's squeaky voice, 'I want my Uncle Pete,' and then there was silence.

'Well,' said Grandad sadly, 'that's the end of that. Come on everyone back into the 'ouse. 2.15 wanted us all to 'ave fun and not grieve and that's what we're goin' to do. We've all suffered a loss but we all benefitted from knowin' 'im too, so I don't want nobody to be an old misery. Come on, Winston, give us a tune and let's all get on with this livin' 'appily ever after caper.'